# Cowboys of the Sky

## Steven C. Levi

# Cowboys
## of the sky

## The Story of Alaska's Bush Pilots

## Steven C. Levi

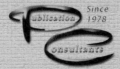

PO Box 221974 Anchorage, Alaska 99522-1974
books@publicationconsultants.com
www.publicationconsultants.com

ISBN 978-1-59433-070-4
First published ISBN 0-827-8331-7

Library of Congress Catalog Card Number: 2008924740

Manufactured in the United States of America

# Dedication

To my niece, Charlotte Chandler Spigner.

*Sometimes the bush pilot needed brute force to get his plane flying. Here Bob Reeve is "adjusting" his plane's propeller with a hammer. [Don't do this on your plane! Bob Reeve was a professional.]* Photo Courtesy of the University of Alaska Anchorage Archives.

There are old pilots and bold pilots,
but there are no old, bold pilots.

… old Alaska Bush pilot flying adage

*Pictured here are four of the leading figures in Kotzebue after the Second World War. On the far left is Bush pilot Gene Jack. Note his pants and boots. This was the style of the day. The man on the far right is John Herbert. Herbert was a wealthy miner from Candle, just across the bay from Kotzebue, and had purchased one of Al Capone's Cadillacs. He gave short rides for a dollar apiece and had plenty of takers. When he tried to bring the Cadillac across to Kotzebue on a barge, the vessel flipped and the car disappeared into the lagoon. Archie Ferguson is next to Herbert and the woman in the picture is Archie's wife, Hadley. Hadley ran the Ferguson flying business from Kotzebue and her verbal fights with Archie over the radio were an ongoing comedy for anyone in the Arctic with a radio.* Courtesy of the University of Alaska Fairbanks.

# CONTENTS

*Damage to a bush plane could happen any time and any where— and often did. Here Bob Reeve's plane is being repaired using a giant tripod near the Ruff & Tuff Mine.* Photo Courtesy of the University of Alaska Anchorage Archives.

# FOREWORD

For Alaskans, flying is like breathing; you have to do it to stay alive. Even in this modern age of speed of light communication, about one-third of Alaska's population still depends on the bush plane. Actually, they don't have a choice. With villages and small communities scattered over an area $\frac{1}{5}$ the size of the Lower 48 and not connected by roads, there were—and still are—only three ways of getting supplies: the once-a-year barge, dogsled and the bush plane.

Flying in Alaska has never been easy. Pilots face some of the worst weather in the world. They set down on landing strips that could be and often are rutted with ice heaves, knee-high in snow or mid-shin deep in mud. Sometimes they land on streams they hope are at least 18 inches deep. In addition to live animals and corpses, they also fly 'missions of mercy' which never seem to come when the weather is good. Their cargo could be as varied as potato chips, dog food and penicillin.

Alaskans grew up with the bush plane. They brought school books in and pregnant women out. In addition to Christmas packages—in and out—they transported public officials from village to village and ministers from congregation to congregation. Law enforcement personnel were flown in and criminals were flown out. And all this was done by men and a few women who were willing to risk their lives to maintain the heartbeat of Alaska.

The Alaska bush pilot is the unsung hero of the north. These 'Cowboys of the Sky' made Alaska what it still is today. They took off into un-flyable weather to save lives and delivered medicine to communities devastated by disease. One at a time they left their mark on the northland. This book is homage to their sacrifice.

*Legendary pilot Joe Crosson, in the mukluks and fur coat, stands on the wing of his plane as Arthur Johnson hands him a cardboard box filled with anti-toxin for a diphtheria epidemic in Point Barrow. Note the wooden crate under the airplane. Though the writing is faint the logo was well-known to Alaska's bush pilots. It is Red Crown Aviation Gasoline. In these early days, gasoline had to be poured into the plane's fuel tanks by hand.* Courtesy of the University of Alaska Fairbanks, Rasmuson Library.

Chapter 1

# ALASKA AND THE BUSH PLANE

IN THE 1920S, DURING THE EARLY DAYS OF THE ALASKA BUSH pilots, it was said that there were three types of weather. The first was *Pan American Weather*. This was because Pan American Airlines was famous for only flying when the sky was as clear as glass. Then there was *Flying Weather* which varied depending on which bush pilot was doing the talking. Finally, there was *Gillam Weather* when flying conditions were so bad that only Harold "Thrill 'em, Chill 'em, Spill 'em, But no Kill 'em" Gillam would fly. The modern term for such weather is *socked in*, meaning that dense fog covers the runway, threatening clouds form a dense ceiling across the sky and there are violent wings that were strong enough to jerk a plane out of the sky.

Whenever there was Gillam Weather, seasoned Alaska bush pilots would sit out the bad spell, primarily because it was too dangerous to fly and, secondarily, in their words, because "God's plenty busy taking care of Harold."[1]

It wasn't that Gillam loved bad weather. It was just that he had no objection to flying in thick soup. He had the eyes of a cat and did not find it difficult to navigate in weather with a visibility of zero. As an example of his ability, in the midst of one particularly brutal night in the late 1930s, a number of Gillam's friends were grounded in McGrath. A storm was blasting with such intensity that, as one of the grounded bush pilots, Oscar Winchell reported, "I wouldn't have whipped a cat out there that night." The pilots were sitting around a fire in a cabin when they heard a plane land. A bit later Gillam walked in, said hello to his friends, fueled his plane and took off. Three days later those same bush pilots were still in McGrath waiting for the storm to lift and Gillam was back in Fairbanks after having safely delivered his mail and supplies.

Gillam was the stuff from which legends are made. But then, so were Alaska's bush pilots, the cowboys of the sky.

"God may have created Alaska," humorist Warren Sitka noted, "but it was the airplane that truly carved the face of the Last Frontier." Few Alaskans would argue with this statement. Seventy years ago—and last year—Alaska's bush pilots carried the groceries, delivered the mail, transported emergency medical personnel, and village-hopped an airborne Santa Claus from Demarcation Point to Unalakleet. Even in an age when Americans have walked on the moon, for villages like Wales, Alexander Creek, or Lake Minchumina, mail still only comes once a week—and that's during the summer.

Alaska is different from the 48 contiguous states, called the *Lower 48* by Alaskans. Ninety percent of Alaska is unreachable by a road. This land mass is called the *Bush* and more than one-third of the population of Alaska lives in this remote area. For these Alaskans, traveling 100 miles is quite different than for anyone else in the United States. In the Lower 48, a trip of 100 miles can be viewed as a little less than two hours by car. The average American climbs into an automobile and then pulls onto a highway or freeway. At 60 miles per hour the driver can leisurely eat up the 100 miles of blacktop in about an hour and forty minutes.

In Alaska, traveling 100 miles can be like stepping back in time. First, even though Alaska is 1/5 the size of the Lower 48, there are fewer than 6,000 miles of paved road, fewer than in a medium-sized city like Riverside, California, El Paso, Texas or Greensboro, North Carolina. Under the best of conditions, a 100 mile trip in Alaska will take significantly longer than one hour and 40 minutes—if the weather is good.

For residents of all bush communities, everything from tooth-picks to prescription drugs must come in by barge or airplane. Barges are efficient when it comes to moving cargo in tons, but very few villages buy many supplies by the ton. When the once-a-year barge does come to a village, the vessel can only arrive during the 120 days a year that the Bering Sea and the rivers are ice-free.

*This is an authentic Alaska gold mine. The metal stack on the right is a steamer. Since the ground is frozen it has to be thawed before it can be dug up one shovel load at a time. Steam is forced into the ground through the pipe you can see in the center of the photograph. Earth that is dug out of the ground to be sluiced for gold is called a "spoil pile" and you can see it on the left side of the photograph.* Photo courtesy of the University of Washington Special Collections.

Even with the bush plane, Alaska communities remain isolated. Historically, this is not unusual. The first Siberians who walked across the Bering Sea Land Bridge 15,000 years ago arrived in an area in which they had no choice but to live in small communities. They lived off the land, much as their ancestors do today.

When the Russian fur traders arrived in the mid-1700s, they struggled with the same problems that plague bush Alaskan today. During the summer, mosquitoes, gnats and biting flies swarmed in clouds and the swampy tundra made transportation overland impossible. Ice covered the Bering Sea eight months a year. When snow shrouded the land and the insects were in hibernation, inland travel was easier, but the low temperatures and long distances between settlements made any journey treacherous.

But the profitable years for the Russian American Company did not last. When the company went bankrupt, the United States bought Alaska for $7.2 million in 1867. While the purchase made the United States the owner of Alaska, the presence of the Federal government was barely felt in the new territory. There were a handful of military governors and scattered pockets of American soldiers. The fur trade continued and, off shore, American whalers plied the waters of the Bering Sea and Arctic Ocean in search of the bowhead whale. For the most part Alaskans were left to fend for themselves.

That all changed with the discovery of gold at the turn of the century. Alaska's two major strikes at Nome and Fairbanks drew 100,000 men and 10,000 women to the northland. The Alaska Gold Rush was unique for two reasons. First, it affected all parts of the territory, from Barrow on the shores of the Arctic Ocean in the north to Ketchikan in the rain forest of Southeast Alaska and Dutch Harbor on the Aleutians. Second, it was one of the longest gold rushes in world history. It began with the discovery of gold in what is now Juneau in 1880s and lasted until the mines shut down during the Second World War.

One of the most important results of the Gold Rush on the history of Alaska was the not only the sudden increase in the population base but the hundreds of small bush communities that sprang to life because of the gold industry. When the town of Nome exploded from a handful of men to full-fledged city of 20,000 residents, it was suddenly economically feasible to ship cargo by the barge-load. As the Gold Rush extended up the Yukon and Kuskokwim Rivers and their tributaries, it became profitable to barge supplies upriver.

*This is Nome's Front Street on the Fourth of July. Note the sign for the Dexter Saloon on the left. This was Wyatt Earp's saloon.* Photo courtesy of the Carrie McClain Museum in Nome.

Even with groceries and building supplies coming in by the ton, the barges still only had 120 days of ice-free travel. There was a railroad in Alaska, which ran from Seward to Fairbanks, but this did little to help the bush communities. Until the coming of the airplane, these villages were supplied by boats during the summer and dogsled during the winter—if they were supplied at all.

*Carl Ben Eielson beside the plane that made history. Eielson's first mail flight cut delivery time between Fairbanks to McGrath from 20 days to two hours.* Courtesy of the Alaska State Library, Harry T. Becker, ASL-P67-154.

Chapter 2

# FLYING BY THE SEAT OF YOUR PANTS

IT WAS THE AIRPLANE THAT BROUGHT ALASKA INTO THE 20th Century. Goods and people could travel farther, faster, making the comforts of civilization available to even the most remote communities. Miners and trappers were assured of a consistent flow of goods and supplies in as was well as the fruits of their labor out. Mail, which had formerly taken ten weeks to reach even the large bush communities from the Pacific Northwest, was now available in hours.

The Golden Age of the Alaska Bush Pilot lasted from the end of the First World War to the beginning of the Second World War. This was an era of very little regulation by the federal government and pilots did more or less as they pleased. The government body that was responsible for air safety, the Civil Aeronautics Administration (CAA), the forerunner of the Federal Aeronautics Administration (FAA), only had a few agents and they were scattered all across Alaska. Because there were few CAA agents, the chances of getting caught with an unsafe airplane were slim. As a result, what is illegal today was commonplace then. Planes flew overloaded, pilots were drunk, and structural damage to the airplanes was fixed with wire, tape and sometimes even tree branches.

From 1917 to 1941, rugged individuals known as bush pilots worked on the very edge of civilization. They faced inclement weather in frail aircraft with undependable engines and made spectacular landings on poor runways—when there were runways—as part of their daily routine. It was an age when men—and some women—truly flew by the "seat of their pants" to maintain the delicate lifeline to the miners, trappers and residents of bush Alaska.

Historically, the first airplane in Alaska was the Tingmayuk. Named after the Eskimo word for bird, the Tingmayuk was a bizarre contraption of 500 pounds of light wood, muslin, and

*Alaska's first airplane.* Photo courtesy of Jim Ruotsala.

piano wire. Built by Professor Henry Peterson, a Nome music teacher, the Tingmayuk was also probably the first airplane in history to be outfitted with skis. The inaugural flight was scheduled for May 9, 1911. On that fateful day, Professor Peterson had the plane pulled out of a shed and dragged to a smooth place on the tundra. Then he climbed aboard and turned on the biplane's gasoline engine. The propeller turned and the plane began inching forward. Unfortunately, that was all it did. When the plane failed to lift off from the level ground, it was taken to a nearby hill and given a push. However, even with a sliding start there was not enough air speed to get the biplane aloft. The next day, the *Nome Nugget* reported "Peterson Unable to Defy the Law of Gravity" and that ended Alaska's first brush with aviation.

Alaskans were first introduced to actual flying two years later. Three Alaskan businessmen contacted James V. Martin, a resident of New England temporarily residing in Seattle, to fly over the ball park during Fairbank's Fourth of July cel-

*Black Wolf Squadron.* **Photo courtesy of the United States Air Force.**

ebration, Martin shipped his aircraft north by steamship to Skagway and then placed the flimsy craft on a railroad flatcar. It was hauled by rail to Whitehorse on the White Pass and Yukon Railway and then the plane went down the Yukon by barge to the Tanana River and Fairbanks. There was no way the Fairbanks businessmen could have predicted the immense success of this first Alaska air show. Hundreds of people jammed the ball park, sat on rooftops, or lined the streets as Martin circled over the town at the fantastic altitude of 200 feet. He flew for 11 minutes and then touched down completing the first flight in Alaska.

In 1920, an event took place that would place Alaska in the aviation book of firsts. On July 15, five officers and three enlisted men from the United States Army took off on the first international cross country flight in history. The crew had been chosen by General Billy Mitchell and was named the Black Wolf Squadron. Commanded by Captain St. Clair Streett, a World War I combat pilot, the squadron entered the Territory of Alaska via Wrangell, crossed over Canada with a stop in Whitehorse and then went on to Nome. Their arrival in Nome completed the flight and marked the first time that the North American continent had been flown by man.

Aviation came to Alaska to stay in 1922 in the form of Carl Ben Eielson. He arrived in Fairbanks to take a job as a school teacher, but flying was in his blood. He had served with the United States Army Air Corps during the First World War and was struck with the possibility of using airplanes to serve the miners, trappers, and villages scattered across Alaska. In those early days of flying in Alaska, the dependable money was in mail delivery. In 1922, a contract to carry the mail was as good as gold.

After badgering postal authorities in Washington, D. C., for more than two years, Eielson was able to convince them to give him a contract to carry mail between Fairbanks and McGrath, a small mining community with a trading post about 250 miles to the west of Fairbanks. The United States Postal Service shipped Eielson a modified De havilland which, with the help of some friends and mechanics, he assembled on a Fairbanks baseball diamond.

Finally he was ready to fly. At 8:50 AM on February 21, 1924, he lifted off the ball park and headed into the crisp Alaska winter. It was five below zero on the ground. Considering Eielson was flying in an open cockpit, it was substantially colder flying at 80 miles an hour above the snow-shrouded Alaska interior.

It was a short flight. At 11:40 AM, Eielson bounced to a stop on the frozen surface of the Kuskokwim River, completing the first air mail delivery in Alaska history. There had been a brief but telling moment when Fred Milligan, who had the dogsled mail contract between Fairbanks and McGrath, looked up in surprise from the dogsled trail as Eielson flew over. "The pilot leaned out and waved at me with his long, black bear skin mittens," Milligan remembered, and at that moment he knew his days on the dogsled mail run were over. It would take Milligan 20 days to reach McGrath, a trip that Eielson was going to complete in a few hours. "I decided then and there," Milligan later recounted, "that Alaska was no country for dogs." Milligan quit dog sledding and went into the airline business, eventually working for Pan American Airlines.

Eielson dropped off his load of mail for McGrath and then collected the 60 pounds of letters and packages to be delivered to Fairbanks. But he made a mistake: he turned off his engine.

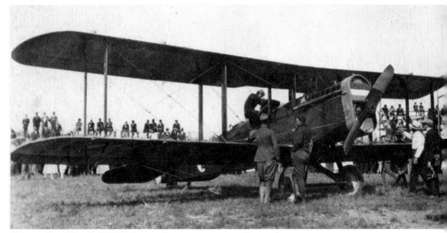

*Here the Black Wolf Squadron meets with enthusiastic spectators at Weeks Field, Fairbanks. This was such a popular photograph it was reproduced as a postcard.* Courtesy of the Anchorage Museum at Rasmuson Center.

As he socialized in McGrath, his engine cooled and when he tried to restart the aircraft, the engine refused to turn over. It took three hours to get the De havilland started again and thus the Fairbanks-bound mail arrived three hours late, a delay that some say the United States Post Office has never made up.

*In the early days of bush flying, plane engines had to be started by hand. Here a pilot cranks the propeller to get the engine started. This photograph was taken in Anchorage, probably on what is now the Park Strip.* Courtesy of the University of Alaska Fairbanks, Rasmuson Library.

Chapter 3

# THE AGE OF EXPERIMENTATION, THE 1920s

THE DAWN OF THE BUSH PILOT CAME IMMEDIATELY AFTER
the First World War. Alaska's population was growing and many
Alaskans had been introduced to the airplane in the United
States Army. Enterprising pilots realized that the airplane could
be used in Alaska to deliver supplies and passenger to the most
remote parts of the territory. The airplane was clearly suited for
Alaska. Most Native villages, mining camps and trap line cab-
ins were hundreds of miles from the nearest railroad. Supplies
were being sent by riverboat and dogsled but with the airplane,
the cargo and mail could be reach their destination in a matter
of hours, not days.

At first the bush planes were used on a charter basis. A mining
operation out of Cordova might need a piece of machinery and
contract with a local pilot. If the pilot was lucky, the machinery
would be light enough so that he could air lift it in one piece.
If not, he had to dismantle the machine and take it in pieces.
If the machine still would not fit, the pilot might have to cut
his plane so that the item would fit inside. After the machinery
had been off loaded, the pilot would repair his plane.

Keeping the mining operations supplied was profitable because the companies needed everything from soda crackers to
ball bearings on a regular basis. The pilots who could not land
a long term contract operated on routes that were established

by need. A pilot might hop to three or four villages picking up and dropping off passengers and cargo along the way. The bulk of the cargo went to the larger villages but passengers could come from anywhere. A trapper might radio to be picked up at a bend of a river or a Native might want to be picked up at a fish camp. Specialty items like fresh fruit, a machine part or a live turkey for Thanksgiving added to the mix of cargo the bush pilots carried.

*In the days before the bush plane, Alaska's mail was sent by dogsled.*
Photo courtesy of the Anchorage Museum Rasmuson Center.

As flying became more attractive, established routes developed. Pilots would live in a transportation hub and fly cargo and passengers as the business developed. Juneau became the hub for Southeast Alaska while Anchorage was the hub for Southcentral Alaska. Fairbanks, which sits in the center of the Interior, provided flight services as far east as the Canada, north to Barrow and the Arctic Ocean, and west to the Bering Sea. Over the years, air routes developed where the business existed, usually between the hubs and the larger bush communities. In the north, the most frequently used routes were between Fairbanks and Barrow, Nome, Kotzebue, and McGrath along with the various mining camps in the Interior. In Southeast Alaska, the main cargo and passenger routes ran between Juneau, as the hub, and Ketchikan, Sitka, Petersburg, and Haines along with the fish canneries which dotted the shoreline. The hub of Anchorage took in the rest of the territory with flights to Cordova, Kenai, Kodiak and out the Aleutian chain.

The Golden Age of the Bush Pilot was a wild time, with pilots stealing each other's passengers and cargo or sending their competitors off on wild goose chases. Archie Ferguson of Kotzebue, who ran the farthest north flying service, was famous for stealing passengers and he was very good at his trade. He would be in the air and hear on the radio that someone in Selawik was asking for Jack Jefford. Archie would beat Jefford into Selawik and tell the passenger that Jefford had "cracked up in Deering." It would only be later that the passenger would realize that he or she had been fooled by the crafty Archie Ferguson.

Archie, it should be added, was also very good at keeping other pilots from stealing his passengers. His wife, Hadley, operated the radio and whenever there was a passengers to be picked up in Deering, she would use a code to say the person was waiting in Shungnak. Anyone trying to steal Archie's passenger could burn a lot of fuel getting to Shungnak only to discover he had been fooled.

In some ways, passenger service in Alaska in the 1920s and 1930s was quite different than it is today. Whether someone liked to fly or not, they flew. They did not have a choice. This aspect of passenger service has not changed in the Bush. But many aspects of bush flying remain the same. Today, as then, many passengers fly on a "call and wait" basis. Passengers would call for their favorite pilot and wait until he or she showed up. There was a great deal of loyalty among passengers to pilots— until something went wrong. Then the loyalty would switch to any carrier. Pilgrim Springs on the Seward Peninsula had a Catholic boarding school and in the late 1930s they would not fly with anyone but Hans Mirow. But that was only until one of Mirow's pilots, Jack Jefford, crashed while taking off. After that, the boarding school people would only fly with Wien.

When a pilot did leave the area, it was not always easy for his replacement to win the loyalty of the old customers. Fred Chambers, a cheechako (tenderfoot) pilot in 1939, learned that when he cracked up in Buckland. He was doing fine until he hit a rut in the runway and knocked off one side of the landing gear. When he got back to Nome, his boss, Hans Mirow, told him, "You've still got your job but I don't know if people will ride with you."

Mirow was right, Chambers learned. Mirow Flying Service would get a call to pick someone up at a mining camp and Chambers would fly out to pick them up. But, recalled Chambers, "they'd see me taxiing and they'd turn around and walk back to camp."

Finding pilots was hard; finding good ones close to impossible. Because of the distance to the Lower 48, particularly from the Arctic, pilots were hired by wire. In those days "when you hired a new pilot you knew it was going to cost you a new airplane," Chambers noted. That was part of the price of doing business in Alaska. You put a new pilot on payroll and pretty soon he was going to "wash out an airplane. You couldn't afford to fire him then because he had learned a valuable lesson at your expense."[2]

But even for the most experienced pilots, flying was dangerous. Being on a plane that went down was not a common occurrence but it was not unusual either. Weather conditions, aviation fuel quality, age of engine parts along with the experience and/or fatigue of the pilot were all part of the formula for keeping a plane aloft. If there was weakness in any one component, the plane could come down. Many did and many people died.

When planes did go down, pilots went to extraordinary attempts to retrieve the damaged craft. Planes were expensive, and it was often more economic to rebuild a damaged aircraft than buy a new one. Considering that a crashed plane was usually in a remote location, salvaging it meant flying a mechanic to the site to do just enough work to get the plane back in the air.

It was not an easy job for the mechanic. It meant camping in a tent at the crash site for weeks. In addition to the grueling work, the mechanics also had to put up with inquisitive bears, meandering moose and mosquitoes that were "pretty near big enough to fly away with yuh," mechanic Jim Hutchison remembered of the weeks he spent in the Bush to repair one particular plane. "I had to use newspapers under my clothes to keep the mosquitoes from biting."[3]

Archie Ferguson is on record for having one of the more dif-

*Anchorage pilot Russ Merrill about to take off from what is now the Anchorage Park Strip. Merrill Field, one of the busiest private airports in America, located in Anchorage, is named in this pilot's honor. Note that the cargo is tied so high on the front that the pilot will have a hard time looking over it.* Photo courtesy of Anchorage Museum Rasmuson Center.

ficult recoveries. After he had gone down on the Hog River, fellow Kotzebue bush pilot John Cross told him "That's one airplane, by God, you'll never fly again."

"Oh, yeah?" snapped Archie who took every challenge seriously. To prove Cross wrong, Archie put together a rescue mission of 20 Eskimos and 72 dogs to drag the airplane almost 300 miles back to Kotzebue where he had it repaired. It did fly again.

As long as no one crashed, passengers stuck to their favorite pilot and would continue to call for a specific person. But the turnover rate for pilots well into the 1950s was high. Often a pilot who had been in Nome in the spring was not there in the fall. He might be flying in another part of the Territory, in a hospital or even dead.

The competition for cargo and passengers was fierce and the rivalry sometimes led to brutal incidents. The sabotaging of landing strips, for instance, was not unknown. Archie Ferguson's chief competitor was Wien Airlines, run by the four Wien brothers. They viewed each other as rivals and Archie was not above adjusting the landing strips when he knew that one of the Wien brothers was on his way in. In these early days, landing strips were anything but convenient. Sometimes they were just level strips of land set aside for planes. Other times they were stretches of beach where someone in the village had stamped out giant letters reading HARD indicated that a landing was possible. During the winter, airstrips were stretches of ice that had been bulldozed level and framed with a dozen flare pots to distinguish the landing area from the rest of the floe. Flare pots, the landing strip lights, were usually just coffee cans full of burning diesel.

During the day, flags stuck in the snow by villagers were placed for the convenience of the pilots. But even with the runway marked, pilots had to be careful. Archie Ferguson once moved the landing strip flags so the next pilot in, Sig Wien, had a very rough landing. After that, Sig gave every landing strip a very careful look before he landed, particularly if he knew Archie had been in the area recently.

For the rest of the pilots, landing was just one of those risks of flying. Sometimes they took off with wheels and found they needed skis to land; or took off with pontoons and found they needed wheels. Mudhole Smith once landed on rocks with skis and Merle Sasseen landed on a golf course with a children's skyride cable wrapped around his landing gear. After a number of such bad landings, Sasseen, known as much for his sense of humor as his flying, was filling out CAA paperwork on his crashes when he came to the question, General Ability as a Pilot? Sasseen thought for a moment and then wrote, "I used to think I was pretty good, but lately I've begun to wonder."

During the early days of bush flying, the number of pilots offering some kind of service was probably no more than 100 hundred. However, more than half of these were men and women who offered an infrequent service. They may have flown friends into remote fishing camps or transported mining equipment for a small operator on a one-time basis. In the 1920s there were probably about 50 pilots who made their living as bush pilots.

But it was a precarious living. Planes and fuel were expensive. Big cargo contracts were few and far between. Revenues in those days were made in three ways: passengers, cargo, and mail. Passengers made up the bulk of the pilot's income with cargo coming in second and mail third. Cargo was not a big money maker because most of the goods bought in the bush came in by barge once a year. Since air lifting supplies was expensive, bush residents often went without an item rather than paying the high cost of flying it in. Mail contracts were highly prized because it was a government contract. The United States government did pay, though it took months to actually get a check. Unfortunately there was not that much mail so the government checks were not that large.

There were other problems pilots had to face as well. After the upkeep of the plane there was the never ending problem of fuel. Few communities had fuel tanks of any kind so all combustibles —including airplane fuel, cooking fuel, fuel oil, and gasoline—came in 55 gallon barrels. The barrels were taken off the barge and stored near the river. This made it easy to service boats that came up the river from the small villages and airplanes that landed on the water. If the community had an airstrip, the 55 gallon drums could be loaded onto a truck and driven out to the airplane.

There were no automatic pumps in those days so the airplane fuel had to be pumped by hand. The cap on the top of the barrel was removed and hand pump installed. Then the pilot would lever the pump handle and force the fuel into his plane's gas tanks. Experienced pilots carried their own chamois to filter aviation gas.

But there were problems. Because many of the tanks were left outside exposed to the weather, the labels on the barrels quickly weathered off and the paint was stripped away. Since the drums were stored all together, unless the operator was careful, he might mistake fuel oil for airplane fuel. Or if the operator wasn't familiar with the operation of an airplane, he might think that gasoline was airplane fuel. There were other matters of concern too. If the airplane fuel drum was left open, water could get into the fuel. Just as bad, mosquitoes and dust could get into the liquid and bring the plane down. One of the strangest stories of airplane crashes in Alaska was when John Cross of Kotzebue had to land on the tundra because his engine suddenly quit. When the plane's engine was examined by a claims adjuster, he discovered a ball of dead mosquitoes had clogged the fuel system. After the corpses of the mosquitoes were removed, the engine worked perfectly.

Perhaps the most visible reminder of this age of aviation is the 55 gallon drum. They were light enough so that they could be lifted by two or three men and transported in a truck or airplane. When they were empty, they could be refilled anywhere fuel was available. Over the years so many were abandoned in remote parts of Alaska that today the 55 gallon drum is nicknamed a Tundra Daisy because, as the old saying goes, "they sprout everywhere."

If there was a pilot who could symbolize this early era, it would be Archie Ferguson. Everyone who met Archie knew everything about him because Archie would tell them. If you didn't know something, Archie would tell you about it whether he knew about it or not. And how he loved to talk. Whether he was on the ground or in the air he was talking, talking, talking. While many of the early bush pilots had sterling reputations of merit, Archie Ferguson was known throughout the northland as Alaska's worst pilot—and possibly the "craziest pilot in the world" as he was dubbed by the Saturday Evening Post. "Maybe he's a pilot," other bush pilots said sadly of Archie, "but he shouldn't be."

Archie Ferguson was a sight to behold. As a young man in Kotzebue he was five foot four and lanky but by the end of the 1930s he was built like a potato. His voice was high pitched and when he laughed, which was often, he cackled like Donald Duck. He only had a few teeth left by the Second World War and kept his dentures in his back pocket —which was a mistake because in one of his crashes, his teeth bit him.

Archie flew primarily in the Arctic, making cargo and passenger runs from Fairbanks to Nome, Kotzebue and every village in between. He had survived more crack-ups than any four pilots combined—as many as two dozen by the Second World War—and he walked away from every one of them. His flying was unorthodox, unpredictable, and a joy to watch—rom the ground.

The best known of Archie's ongoing escapades was the *Arctic Bump*. As far as Archie was concerned, a trip without excitement was not a trip worth taking and he was very good at making his own excitement. On trips across the Arctic Circle he would tell newcomers that there was no air over that theoretical line on the earth.

"We're comin' ta the Arctic Circle!" he would yell at his passengers as he surreptitiously turned off his gas. "Ya can't see it but ya'll sure know when we hit it. The engine'll quit! There's no air in that darn circle for eight hundred feet!"

The plane's engine would then sputter and die and the plane would fall for hundreds of feet, the passengers shrieking in terror. After he had his laugh, Archie would quietly switch the fuel back on, re-start the engine and continue of his way.

Today, Alaska's pilots keep this tradition alive. While they don't allow the plane to fall hundreds of feet, they will give the plane an extra blast of fuel to make it bump when they come to the Arctic Circle.

Archie's primary competitors were the Wien brothers. They started Wien Airlines and were known for their caution and flying precision. While the best pilots refused to take unnecessary risks, some took no risks at all. At the head of this pack was Sig Wien. Sig would fly only under the best of conditions. Like most other pilots, he flew only in daylight. When it started to get dark, he landed. If the weather closed in, he stayed until it cleared. But Sig took his caution to the extreme. While flying an Arctic route, Wien personnel sometimes wouldn't know where he was for days at a time. He would land in a village that had no radio and there he would sit, waiting for the weather to lift.

Alaska's bush pilots also made an international mark in aviation in this era as well. Hubert Wilkins came north in 1928 and convinced Carl Ben Eielson to join him in his quest to be the first to circumnavigate the Polar Basin. Eielson agreed and the trip almost cost both men their lives. The pair left Barrow in a Lockheed Vega on April 15, 1928, and followed the curvature of the earth toward Greenland. Twenty hours and 20 minutes later—the longest, nonstop airplane flight in the Arctic—they were forced to land near Spitsbergen because of storm conditions. For five days the men sat in their Vega waiting for the weather to lift. When it did, the snow was so deep the plane could not take off. Marooned hundreds of miles from any help, the men might have joined the ranks of those who had flown off into the Arctic and never returned. But luck was on their side.

After they had stamped out a crude runway, Wilkins tried pushing the plane to get it started. He was successful but could not make it aboard when the plane took off. Eielson landed and they tried again. And again. On the third time, Wilkins was able to give the Vega enough of a push to get it started down the runway and, at the same time, hook his leg in the entry hatch of the plane. As the plane was taking off he was able to lever himself aboard with a piece of driftwood he had picked up from a nearby beach. Considering that the Vega was low on fuel when the men were forced down, it is quite likely that had they not made it into the air when they did, they might not have had the gas to reach a refueling station. When they completed their trip, they had traveled 2,200 miles around the polar basin, the first men to do so.

While exploration was great for press headlines, it did not keep food on the pilot's table. Flying was a business and the pilot had to show a profit. Just as important as flying passengers was the transport of cargo. In the 1920s, and today, bush cargo was a mix of products, some living and some so bulky they had to be taken apart to fit inside. If the plane was too full, pilots sometimes lashed cargo on the outside. Sig Wien remembered flying a bed spring outside his plane. Other pilots had horror stories of timber and pipe that had to be strapped to the fuselage of their planes. Some of the photos of early aircraft show them so bulky with

*Because cash was so hard to come by the Bush, stores became minting their own money. The coins, called bingles, were legal if they could only be redeemed at the store that issued them. But no one followed that rule and soon bingles were being used as coins all across the Bush. That's when they were made illegal by the United States Department of the Treasury.* Photo courtesy of Danny Daniels.

cargo strapped to the outside that it was a wonder the plane ever lifted off at all. Once in the air, it is surprising that the pilot could see over the cargo tied to the front of the aircraft.

Bush pilots could—and often did—transport anything. Transporting walrus to zoos in the Lower 48 was not unusual. "They'd cry real tears when they'd be aboard because they were stressed and it just hurt your feelings," remembered K Doyle, the first stewardess for Wien Air Alaska. Horses and dogs were not uncommon in the larger planes and once in the 1950s Wien Air Alaska flew an elephant to Nome—but in a larger cargo plane.

The proper loading of cargo was critical to the balance of the plane. Strapping down the cargo was important as well. Russ Merrill, for whom Merrill Field in Anchorage is named, learned about shifting cargo the hard way. He left Anchorage in a Whirlwind Travelaire on September 16, 1929, with a compressor for a gold mine. He never returned. The only clue as to what happened was a piece of fabric that was found floating in Cook Inlet that was identified as being from his airplane. It was speculated that the compressor had shifted while he was in flight and the imbalance sent the plane tumbling into the Inlet.

Archie Ferguson, of course, had his own cargo stories. Once in the 1920s, he alleged, he flew a load of turkeys from Nome to Kotzebue. He couldn't get the turkey crates into his Cessna Air Master so he took the turkeys out of the crates and put them into his cargo hold individually. As Archie told it, he had trouble taking off so he began waving his hand in the cargo bay behind him. This upset the turkeys and they started flying around in the back of the plane. This enabled Archie to take off. Once aloft, Archie kept waving his hand to keep some of the turkeys in flight all the time and was able to make it all the way to Kotzebue without incident. While this is certainly a humorous story, the fact of the matter is that domesticated turkeys don't fly. But then again, a lot of bush pilots said Archie couldn't fly either.

Chapter 4

# THE TECHNOLOGICAL AGE, THE 1930s

BY THE END OF THE 1920S, THE AVIATION BUSINESS WAS profitable enough to attract more pilots into the industry. But there was now a new breed of pilot. While many of the original class of bush pilots had grown up in Alaska, the new pilots came from Outside. Many of them had years of flying experience. But it was still flying experience in the Lower 48, not in Alaska.

Once in Alaska skies, these newcomers quickly learned what the seasoned Alaska bush pilots already knew. It was a "long way between places" with few places to set the plane down if there was an emergency. Navigation equipment was still primitive. Days were short above the Arctic Circle, particularly during winter. Accurate maps were rare, except for nautical charts which were only useful if a pilot was flying along the coastline.

The newer pilots also had to learn that many of the basic rules of navigation were different in Alaska. In the Arctic the sun didn't rise in the east during the winter; it came up in the south. Compass readings changed as well. Magnetic North and True North, which were virtually the same to a pilot in Arizona or Louisiana, were substantially different to an aviator in the Arctic. The further north the pilot flew, the greater the disparity between the two points grew.

Then there was the weather. Southeast Alaska was famous for its violent wind, called a Taku. During the winter wind from off the Pacific Ocean would blast up the narrow channels of Southeast Alaska. As the wind is funneled it grows in strength with gusts of well over 100 miles an hour, strong enough to blow cars over, sink ships and make flying extremely dangerous. Along the Aleutian Islands, the powerful wind is called a williwaw. A williwaw is particularly dangerous because it often rises from calm skies. One moment the weather appears clear and clam and the next, a 100 knot wind is blasting across an island. This is particularly dangerous for an airplane that is landing. In the rest of Alaska, wind shears are not uncommon, rain *as thick as a wall* can cut visibility to zero feet and low-lying fog can obscure coastlines.

The most experienced pilots from the Lower 48 quickly learned to adjust their flying to the weather. Many pilots used the power of the wind to their advantage. If the wind constant over the landing strip, the pilots will face their planes into the wind and then cut back on the power. As they cut back on more and more power, the plane will gentle settle to the ground. Conversely, on take off, the pilots will face their planes into the wind and add just enough power to rise off the ground vertically. Under these conditions it is possible take off using zero feet of runway.

But it was flying during the winter that separated the professionals from the amateurs. The brutal Alaska climate forced pilots to develop new ways of thinking about flying. In Anchorage and Fairbanks, there could be snow on the ground as early as the middle of October and stay until mid-May. Many pilots could not stand the cold and the flying conditions that winter brought and fled south as soon as the lakes and streams began to freeze over.

Winter always brought treacherous conditions. Along with snow and ice came the extremely low temperatures, particular in the Arctic and the Interior. Even the most experienced pilots considered the cold an enemy of the aircraft. It affected the plane, its flying ability and, most notably in Fairbanks, landing conditions.

Fairbanks sits in a geologic bowl surrounded by hills. On many winter days temperature inversions make it far colder at ground level than at 12,000 feet. Under normal conditions, it gets colder the higher a plane flies. But when there is a temperature inversion, the coldest weather is on the ground. A pilot at 2,000 feet might be flying in a temperature of 10 below zero but, as soon as the pilot descended, the plane would drop into the cold belt of air lying on the ground. The thick blanket of air over the landing strip could be 50 degrees below zero. While the pilot in a relatively warm cockpit might not register the change in temperature, the plane's engine most certainly would.

"On the air-cooled engines," remembered Robert Jacobson, mechanic and pilot for Alaska Airlines and MarkAir until his retirement in 1985, "the engine would sometimes freeze. Here you were coming in for a landing and the engine would quit on you at 100 feet. If you weren't lined up for a landing, you were dead."[4]

Jacobson solved this problem with a bit of new technology. In the late 1940s he invented a cowling flap system which forced cold air to circulate around the hot engine before it was used to cool the engine. Only in Alaska, he noted, would you have to heat the air before you used it for cooling.

Cold weather also brought on the problem of icing. Icing is the process where moisture in the air comes in contact with an airplane and turns to ice. An example would be a pilot flying at 5,000 feet where it is raining. When he dropped to 3,000 feet he discovers that the temperature is below freezing. All of the rain that was on his plane would now be ice and freezing rain from the 5,000 foot level would coat his plane thicker and thicker as the sheet of ice grew in thickness. This is very dangerous because ice affects lift and adds weight to a plane. With each passing moment, the plane picks up weight and has less lift. If it picks up too much weight and loses too much lift, it will become unable to remain aloft and the plane will tumble out of the sky.

Archie Ferguson learned this lesson the hard way. Heavily loaded and icing up, he clipped a tree on the Hog River.

"That was certainly close," his passengers muttered.

"Sure was," replied Archie peering through his windshield, "but those two trees up there are the ones that are going to stop us." He pointed ahead to a pair of trees coming up fast.

Overloaded with cargo on the inside and ice on the outside, as Archie predicted, his plane hit the trees and tumbled to the ground.

*Not all bush flights ended on a runway. Here Archie Ferguson landed in a swamp on the Hogg River. He was marooned for several days until help was able to arrive. The only injury in the crash was Ferguson's ego.* Photo courtesy of Ed Yost.

Today, all passenger planes and some private planes are equipped with de-icing equipment. This equipment includes an alcohol/water mixture that is used on the windshield to keep them clear. This mixture is also allowed to trickle down the propellers from the hub. As the prop spins, the alcohol/water mixture sheets blades and maintains an ice-free surface of the rotor. For the wings, inflatable sections are installed on the leading edge where icing usually starts. Before ice builds, the inflatable sections are pressurized causing the front of the wing to expand. After ice forms, the tubes are deflated and the ice breaks free. Then, as ice forms on the deflated tubes, they are inflated breaking the ice free. This process continues as long as the plane is in icing danger.

One of the best known pilots of this era was Harold "Thrill 'em, Chill 'em, Spill 'em, But no Kill 'em" Gillam. He was the embodiment of the ideal Alaska bush pilot. He was a dashing, handsome man with rugged features and a personality to match. Once, when some school children were asked to write a poem about their favorite person, a third grader in Cordova wrote five lines that became Gillam's nickname for life:

> He thrill 'em
> Chill 'em
> Spill 'em
> But no kill 'em
> Gillam

Gillam started in the flying business in 1931 as part of the cargo supply line between Cordova and dozens of mining operations in the nearby mountains. It was a risky operation on the best of days. Cordova sits on a flat plain surrounded on three sides by steep mountains. On the fourth side is Orca Inlet which connects with the Gulf of Alaska. Turbulent winds and fog are common in the area and storm clouds were considered a normal weather pattern. Adding to a pilot's woes, most of the landing strips at the mines were very short and some were actually areas that had been dug out of the mountainside with bulldozers. Landing and taking off were treacherous. "If you undershot," the seasoned bush pilots said of the area, "you ran into a bluff. When you took off you hadn't a foot to spare."

But even in this country, it appeared that nothing could keep Gillam on the ground. One night Honest John McCreary fell in his cellar and was badly gouged by a nail. There was a blasting snowstorm and those who attended his wounds believed that McCreary would die because there was no way to get him to the nearest doctor, at Kennecott 125 miles away. But the storm didn't bother Gillam. Loading Mc-Creary into his airplane, Gillam battled driving winds and snow to get him to the doctor. When the doctor said that McCreary probably wouldn't last the night, Gillam went up again, flying back to Cordova to fetch McCreary's son and then flew back to Kennecott. That night Gillam flew 375 miles through a driving snowstorm and cemented his reputation as a man who had the eyes of a cat.

*Carl Ben Eielson.* Courtesy of the University of Alaska Fairbanks, Rasmuson Library.

Gillam remained in Cordova for three years and then went north to Fairbanks where his reputation as an aviation marvel continued to grow. He was best known for his night flying. Regardless of the weather, Gillam would rise in the evening, dress and then fly to wherever he was scheduled to go. In 1938, Gillam had the mail contract between Fairbanks and 20 bush communities. For the previous few years these villages had been serviced by Pan American Airlines, but the mail had been delivered only when the weather was good. Gillam delivered the mail on time, month after month, season after season, with a perfect safety record. Gillam's record of deliveries on time was so good that the United States Post Office declared it to be the best in the United States and its territories—better than in places like Kansas or Arizona where the weather was more predictable and the terrain more suited to emergency landings.

Alaska pilots accepted Gillam's flying exploits as fact because they watched Gillam perform feats of navigational witchcraft. But pilots from other parts of the country didn't believe a word of Gillam's exploits. In the mid-1930s, one man, Donneld Cathcart, was so convinced that Alaskans were lying about Gillam's talents that he rode with Gillam between Fairbanks and Barrow.

Gillam fueled his Fairchild Pilgrim with 7 hours worth of fuel - for the 6 1/2 hour trip—and the two men scrambled aboard. As far

*Harold "Thrill 'em, Chill 'em, Spill 'em but no Kill 'em" Gillam.* Photo courtesy of the Reeve family.

as Cathcart could see, Gillam had no navigation equipment. The Pilgrim leaped into the air and chewed its way up through several thousand feet of cloud cover and proceeded to fly over a sea of clouds for six and a half hours. Then, without warning, Gillam nosed the plane back down into the cloud bank.

43

In the next instant the Pilgrim was enveloped in the clouds. Down and down the plane went and no matter where he looked, Cathcart could see nothing but clouds in every direction. Suddenly he did see something flash by the Fairchild's windshield. It was the antenna poles marking the landing area on the Barrow Lagoon. Gillam made a perfect landing. Cathcart was forced to believe that Gillam's reputation was not only true but well earned.

Archie Ferguson was still flying in the 1930s and continuing to add to his legacy. In the late 1930s, he was transporting two baby polar bears when they got loose in his aircraft. Archie didn't know the cubs were loose until one of them hit him on the back of his head. Everyone on the ground knew Archie was in trouble when he came on the air and began shrieking that bears were loose in his plane and were going to eat him alive. For the next twenty minutes, Archie kept everyone within radio range tuned in to his battle with the bear cubs. He landed in Kotzebue so perfectly that it was said by more than one of his competitors that one of the bears must have been at the controls.

Another non-Alaskan pilot who has his name etched in the history of Alaska aviation is Wiley Post. After the hubbub over Charles Lindbergh flying across the Atlantic to Paris in 1927, aviators set their signs on a new goal—a flight around the world. The Graf Zepplin had circled the globe in 21 days but Wiley Post, even then a famed American aviator, estimated that he could do it by airplane in ten days. On June 23, 1931, Post and Australian aviator Harold Gatty left Roosevelt Field, Long Island, in a Lockheed Vega named the Winnie Mae. Eight days, 15 hours and 51 minutes later the Winnie Mae landed after circumnavigating the earth in record time.

But Post felt he could do it even faster. Two years later, on July 15, 1933, the Winnie Mae left Floyd Bennett Field in New York. But this time Post was flying alone. Using an automatic pilot—which he had invented—he flew nonstop to Berlin and proceeded across Russia and the Bering Sea. Once over Alaska he became lost in Alaska's legendary bad weather. Spotting a radio tower poking through the cloud cover, he landed on the rough 800 foot runway at the mining community of Flat. The moment he hit the air strip he was in grave danger. The Winnie Mae nosed over on its prop and the landing gear on the right side snapped off.

Now, with his around-the-world-solo record in jeopardy, the miners of Flat rushed to his rescue. While Post got some badly

*This is a photograph of the first plane to fly around the world. Here it is refueling in Sitka.* Photo courtesy of Jim Ruotsala.

needed sleep, the miners worked through the night to make what repairs they could and radioed for spare parts from Fairbanks. When the Winnie Mae was flyable, Post flew to Fairbanks for more extensive repairs. With the assistance of the miners at Flat and the mechanics in Fairbanks, Post was able to circle the globe alone in a record 7 days, 18 hours and 49 minutes.

Wiley Post left a grim legacy in the northland as well. In February of 1935, he purchased a hybrid Lockheed Orion-Explorer and outfitted the craft with pontoons from another plane, a Fairchild 71. That August, American humorist Will Rogers joined Post for a leisurely flight to Alaska. The two men arrived in Fairbanks to refuel on their way to Barrow to visit Charlie Brower, the self-styled *King of the Arctic*. With the Orion-Explorer tanks partially filled to let the plane take off from the waters of the Chena River, the two men left for Barrow.

By the early afternoon the men were lost above the cloud cover in one of the worst storms for that time of year for years. About 3:00 Post spotted some land and trees through a break in the

*Wiley Post and Will Rogers only hours before they crashed outside of Barrow. The man on the far right is legendary Alaska Bush pilot Joe Crosson. Wiley Post has the patch over his eye. The small man is Leonard Seppala, the man who ran the last leg of the Serum Run into Nome to save the population from diphtheria in 1925.. To-day, the Iditarod dog sled race is in commemoration of that Serum Run.* Photo courtesy of Jim Ruotsala.

clouds and dropped through the cloud cover. He followed a stream until it came to a lagoon large enough for the Orion to land. There was a small Inupiat Eskimo fish camp on the shore of the lagoon where Post was given precise directions to Barrow, 16 miles away. Post and Rogers talked for a moment and then disappeared back in the Orion. The plane took off, rose 50 feet off the water and suddenly the engine quit. The plane took a nose dive into the lagoon and, in the next instant, both men were killed. Claire Okpeaha, one of the Eskimos on the lagoon, ran the 16 miles to Barrow with the bad news. Later, Okpeaha would report that Rogers only said one thing to him as he stuck his head out of the Orion: "Anyone here from Paducah?" Other than his conversation with Post, those were Rogers' last words. What was particularly tragic was that Post and Rogers had died of pilot error: the plane had simply run out of gas. When the gas tanks were probed with a stick, they were found to be bone dry.

As Post and Rogers proved, flying could be deadly. Pilots had to be ever alert to changing circumstances, even if they were sure they were operating safely. Landing and takeoffs could be dangerous. In the late 1930s, Merle Mudhole Smith was flying for Cordova Air Service and one of his clients was the Bremmer Mining Company. The mine was in a very inaccessible spot for a airplane—

*Claire Okpeaha, the Inupiat Eskimo who watched as Wiley Post crashed into the lagoon.* Photo courtesy of Bill Bacon.

its air strip was 300 feet long, barely 20 feet wide, had a ditch on each side, and was covered with stones.

After a driving rainstorm, Smith arrived at the mine to drop off supplies. As he was loading up to return to Cordova, one of the miners advised him to check the landing strip to make certain that he had not dislodged any rocks when he had landed. If he had, there would have been a pothole in the runway which would have made his take off hazardous. Merle said he was sure he hadn't flipped any rocks large enough to be a danger so checking the runway was not necessary.

*Archie Ferguson.* Photograph courtesy of Edith Bullock.

He was wrong.

As he started to take off, the left wheel on his Stearman dropped into a mudhole that had formed after his tail wheel had dislodged a rock during the landing. The Stearman buckled and bounced nose down, the propeller boring into the ground at 1800 revolutions a minute. Thereafter Merle Smith was known as Mudhole Smith.

Sometimes even the best prepared pilot could find himself in trouble In Southeast Alaska, Tony Schwamm was landing a water plane on what he thought was deep water. His pontoons touched the water and he started to glide to a stop when suddenly he felt himself being lifted skyward. When he looked out his side window he realized that his plane was on the back of a whale. Once the whale realized he had a plane on its back, it went back down leaving Schwamm with a story that will live forever in the annals of Alaska bush flying.[5]

Another tale of a pilot being lifted after a landing comes from the life of Bob Reeve. Reeve once landed on a field outside of Dawson, Yukon Territory, and sent a team of two horses pounding into a barn in fright. As he was helping the farmer extricate the horses from the tangle of rope and harness, the horse that had fallen on the ground kicked the horse that was standing. And the horse that was standing kicked Reeve sending him flying "a good 20 feet."[6]

Another bush pilot who left his mark on Alaska aviation in the 1930s was Alex Holden of Alaskan Southern Airways. Though he had a career that spanned many decades, Holden is most often remembered for what is laughingly called the Great Corpse Rush.

During the Great Depression a fisherman in Dutch Harbor died. A death certificate was issued by the United States Marshal and the next of kin was notified courtesy of some letters which were found among the old man's possession. One of those documents was the fisherman's will, in which he left his entire estate, estimated at $1.4 million in 1990 dollars, to a niece in Washington. She decided that his corpse should be transported back to Seattle.

Since the cadaver was 900 miles west of Seward, the closest ferry terminal, the woman offered several thousand dollars to any pilot who would fly to Dutch Harbor and bring the corpse to the ferry terminal. During the Depression, a few thousand dollars could mean the difference between life and death for a small airline, so more than a few pilots tried to reach Dutch Harbor. The first to arrive was Alex Holden.

But as he quickly discovered, he got more than he bargained for. The fisherman had died of complicated internal conditions, which required that his remains be disposed of promptly. To make matters worse, the body had already been buried. To recover the corpse, Holden would need an exhumation order to get the body out of the ground. But there was no judge in Dutch Harbor. Holden wired his boss of the complications and asked for instructions. The reply he received was short and to the point: "Get the body."

Holden then got an exhumation order from a judge in Anchorage by radio and had the body dug up. As quickly as possible Holden had the body wrapped in a canvas shroud and several coats of shellac applied to seal in the corpse.

After the shellac had dried, Holden discovered there was no way to slide the mummy into his plane. The cadaver couldn't be bent and Holden couldn't maneuver the stiff cargo through the cargo door. Even if he had been able to cut a hole in the side of the airplane and slip the corpse in, the stench of shellac would have made the trip unbearable. After trying every cargo loading trick he knew, Holden finally bowed to the inevitable and strapped the corpse onto the top of a wing and flew it to Seward.

*Cover of the biography of Harold Gillam, Sr. by Arnold Griese.* Courtesy of Publication Consultants.

Chapter 5

# THE CAA ARRIVES, THE 1940s

IF THERE WAS A DATE THAT MARKED THE END OF THE WILD and woolly days of rough-and-tumble competition it was the Fall of 1938. After years of loosely watching bush pilots, the CAA (Civil Aeronautics Administration) decided to regulate the industry. (The CAA was the forerunner of today's Federal Aviation Administration, the FAA.) Announcing that it intended to assign routes on the basis of "convenience and necessity," the CAA sent its inspectors to Alaska to see which routes should be assigned. This was a polite way of saying that the CAA was going to decide who had a monopoly on which routes.

The pilots were not pleased with the idea of regulation coming to Alaska and called a mass meeting to discuss the matter among themselves. This proved to be a bad idea. It was, reported Ray Petersen of Northern Consolidated, (later Wien), "like a bunch of lions and panthers tossed in one cage!"[7] For the first time, every pilot in Alaska was going to come face-to-face with every one of his competitors. As soon as all the pilots were in the same room they decided that their competitors were a greater threat to their livelihood than government regulations and after some heavy drinking, a wild brawl erupted. That finished any hope of the pilots standing as a solid front against the CAA. Just as the coming of barbed wire symbolized the end of the cowboy, the coming of the CAA ended the frontier days of the bush pilot.

After examining the routes, the CAA decided to assign the airways on the basis on who had been flying there. If a pilot had been servicing an area for the period between May 14, and August 22, 1938, he would be assigned that service route. This grand fathering caught some of the pilots without a route. Though Bob Reeve had been flying in the Valdez area for years, during the three months the CAA chose as their window, he

*Jim Robbins.* Photo Courtesy of the Robbins Family.

had been doing aerial mapping in Fairbanks. So Reeve didn't get a route. On the other hand, Ray Petersen had been working out of Bethel at the time and, because he had a girlfriend in Anchorage, he had been flying back and forth between the two communities frequently. So he got the Bethel to Anchorage route, "the only reason I had an airline," he later noted.[8]

The arrival of the CAA in Alaska was both a blessing and a

curse. It was not so much that the CAA brought new technology to Alaska. Rather, the organization brought a hard nosed approach to federal regulations. Planes would not be allowed to fly overloaded. Every airline and pilot would have to maintain their equipment and engines to federal standards and standard equipment was routinely checked to make sure it worked. Pilots who installed broken equipment just to meet the federal requirements soon discovered that the CAA was serious about making every plane safe.

Along with that technology came a growing number of CAA inspectors. From the pilot's point of view, this was not a step forward. As far as the pilots were concerned, the CAA was evil incarnate and it was hated with ferocity. Pilots did not look at the CAA as a safety-oriented agency but as a bureaucracy full of incompetents intent on putting pilots out of business. Pilots had good reason to be concerned about CAA motives. The small airlines had their hands full just struggling to survive. Now the agency was requiring them to keep books, maintain equipment and not overload their planes.

The CAA was supposedly in Alaska to make sure that the pilots flew safely. But the way the agency enforced regulations ensured that almost no one could stay in business and still follow CAA regulations. At least that was how the pilots saw it. From the CAA's point of view, the inspectors were usually amazed at the condition of Alaska airplanes. They wondered how the crates could even get off the ground, much less fly cargo and passengers. Many of the pilots were flying without radios or fire extinguishers. Overloading was common, equipment failure was frequent and engine maintenance was slipshod.

Thus pilots played a cat-and-mouse game with the CAA, dodging the inspectors while the CAA tried to catch them unaware. If it had not been so serious, it would have been comical. In Kotzebue, when the CAA tried to pull a snap inspection, invariably every pilot who could fly had flown the coop by the time the inspector arrived. Whenever a plane crashed on take-off, it was a race to see who got to it first: the CAA with a set of scales to weigh the cargo or every other pilot on the airstrip. The pilot's buddies would be busy helping the unlucky airman unload his plane so the CAA inspector would not find that the plane had been grossly overloaded. Once Don Emmons went off the runway at Weeks' Field in Fairbanks and by the time the CAA inspectors got there the only cargo left aboard was "about two cases of beans."[9]

Understandably, the CAA had a rough time enforcing its hated regulations, but CAA activities did have a noticeable impact on flying in Alaska. Just as the State Trooper who sits visibly along the interstate slows traffic simply by being there, the CAA changed aviation in Alaska just by showing a presence.

Sometimes pilots had good reason to ignore CAA regulations. The weight limits for legal loads were quite strict, and pilots carrying full tanks of fuel had a very narrow margin for cargo. Even Burleigh Putnam, who headed the CAA in Alaska during the 1940s, admitted that "payload didn't mean a thing. Our own CAA airplane, when it was full of gasoline, could only carry 20 pounds legally and I flew it one time with a 1,050 pound overload."[10]

Most pilots fudged on their poundage when they flew cargo loads. Even after the CAA moved maximums up to more reasonable levels, pilots continued to overload their airplanes. There was a good reason for the fudging—profit. The bigger the load, the greater the profit. Overloading was often not just a result of greed; it was a matter of keeping the airline companies solvent.

Ray Petersen of Northern Consolidated later known as Wien Consolidated, in a conversation with Beth Day, author of *Glacier Pilot*, made the truest statement regarding overloading in the early days:

> Our loads were determined by the length of the field and whether we could make it off the ground. We'd fill up all the seats, throw in all the freight our passengers' laps would hold, fill up the gas tanks,

and take off. On a long trip we could take an extra load because as the gas burned out we got the additional lift we needed to make it over a pass. When the CAA Inspector was around, we'd wait until he went to lunch, then everybody would overload their planes and take off fast.

But there was great danger in overloading. Many pilots thought they knew the safety limits and would still throw in an extra box. After all, it was only a box. The next time it was

*Ray Petersen.* Photo courtesy of Wien Collection.

two boxes or a heavy bag. It was, as Ray Petersen noted, "that last ten bucks worth of freight" that killed the pilot. Maybe he needed more feet of runway then he had and went off the landing strip into the trees. Or he increased his stall speed so that he, quite literally, fell out of the sky on final approach.

Sometimes the plane had to be cut to accommodate the cargo. In the summer of 1949, polar bear hunter Harold Little watched as Archie Ferguson, "jammed a boiler into his Fairchild 24. The boiler was in Point Lay and Archie wanted that boiler in his plane in the worst way. When the boiler wouldn't fit, Archie chopped a hole in the roof of the Fairchild and flew it with the stove pipe sticking through the top of the airplane."

Other tales of overloading have a trace of humor. Merle Mudhole Smith, known to be cantankerous upon occasion, once loaded up a plane and sent a young pilot, Ralph Westover, into the sky. "The plane was overloaded and packed with boxes from door to door," Westover recalled. He made it off the ground but when he returned, Mudhole was in a rage. "You had another hundred feet of runway," Mudhole snarled. "You could have taken another hundred pounds of cargo!"[11]

*Merle Mudhole Smith.* Photo courtesy of the Smith family.

Prior to the 1950s, on smaller planes, cargo meant revenue so it went aboard first. Passengers often sat on top of the sacks and boxes. Many of the pilots preferred cargo to passengers because, as glacier pilot Bob Reeve put it succinctly, "Cargo don't talk back."

Flying passengers was often financially risky for everyone concerned. If a pilot had to fly a carpenter out to a construction site, often the carpenter had to fly first and wait for his tools to catch up to him. This was terribly expensive for the construction company because the carpenter could not work if he did not have his tools with him— yet he would still have to be paid since he was on the construction site. Certainly he could borrow tools, but a carpenter without his own tools was only half-efficient. If that carpenter was a specialist, he might have to sit around on payroll until his gear caught up with him and that would be expensive for his employer.

The bad news for the employer could get worse if the weather closed in. Then the carpenter would be sitting for days, on payroll, waiting for his tools. This set of circumstances did not endear the flying service to the construction company.

Sometimes passengers could be a problem. Don Emmons was taking his common law wife to Fairbanks when she apparently decided to commit suicide. Halfway to Fairbanks she opened the door and stepped out into thin air. At the last moment, another passenger caught her by the foot and held on tightly. However, since the woman was hanging lower than the wheels, Emmons had no choice but to order her dropped before he landed. She fell into a deep snow bank and was rescued by dog sledders shortly thereafter.

Bill Munz, flying out of Nome, even showed how an airplane could do double duty and help a dog team. In December of 1945, he was north of Teller flying a pregnant woman into Nome when he spotted a herd of reindeer being chased by a runaway dog sled. He followed the coastline until he came across Frank Ahnangatoguk stranded four miles behind his dog team. Munz picked him up and then flew back to the dog team. There he "executed a treacherous landing between the dog team and the reindeer herd, thus stopping the team." Ahnangatoguk got out and Munz landed in Nome shortly thereafter. But by then he had an extra passenger on board: the pregnant woman had given birth before he made it to Nome.

While the dirty, rusted aircraft that flew the Alaska Bush may have been considered primitive by many Lower 48 pilots, the planes were remarkably dependable. In the Territory, a plane was not just a vehicle that moved people and cargo from one place to another. It was a life-line and a life-saver. But it took more than a pilot to make the trip. Mechanics were as critical as the pilots. Quite a bit of sweat and precision went into maintaining the aircraft, from the engine block to the fuselage skin. But it was not in vain. When Walter Beech of Beechcraft was in Kotzebue in 1941 he told the Alaska aviators that the stitch Eskimo women had done on the fabric of the planes in the Arctic was better than that done by machines in his factory! Beech also endeared himself to Alaskans by his comment concerning the Beech Travelaire, one of the most dependable planes in the sky. "Well, damn it all, I designed 'em right," he said in Cordova, "and they should still be flying."[12] Some of them are still flying today.

*Don Emmons at Week's Field in Fairbanks.* Photo courtesy of Jim Ruotsula.

But all this technology did not translate into better flying conditions. The weather was still unpredictable. Arctic weather still closed in suddenly and remained unflyable for days. Sometimes good flying weather would self-destruct so quickly that pilots would be forced to land wherever they were and wait for the clouds to lift. Sometimes the pilots didn't get that chance. In the mid-1950s, Jefford was flying between Golovin and Elim in Northwest Alaska when he was caught in a powerful down draft and suddenly felt "an awful jar on the airplane." Not sure what had happened, he began easing back on the throttle.

Nothing happened so he eased back another increment.

Again he felt no difference in his flying so he eased back on the throttle again.

He kept easing back on the throttle and feeling no effect until he realized that he could not possibly be flying.

So he turned his engine off.

When the weather cleared he found himself perched on a mountain top. There he stayed for seven days waiting to be rescued.

Archie Ferguson also had his problems with the weather. In December of 1946, Archie Ferguson was flying his neighbor, Bess Cross, back to Kotzebue. Following Archie was a second plane carrying Cross' $2,500 fur coat along with a case of Scotch whiskey, several pounds of pork chops and a load of vegetables for Cross' store, the Kotzebue Trading Post.

As the two planes headed out along the Bering Sea coast, the second pilot lost Archie in the fog. Then a weather front moved in and the pilot was forced to land on a sand bar to wait for the cloud cover to pass. Seven days later, when Archie found him, the pilot was sitting bundled up in Cross' fur coat and guzzling her whiskey. He had already devoured every one of her pork chops and all of the produce.

Until the end of the Second World War, most pilots did not use instruments. Today, there are two ways to fly: VFR (Visual Flight Rules) and IFR (Instrument Flight Rules). In the Golden Era of the Bush Pilots, most aviators flew by line of sight. When new instruments became available, the older pilots shied away from using them. If a cheechako asked an old Bush pilot if he flew VFR or IFR, the pilot would sometimes jokingly say:

"IFR" an acronym to veteran pilots for I Fly the River or I Follow the Railroad.

But technology, particularly in the form of navigation equipment, could keep the pilots alive. While folklore had it that Gillam "hadn't a nerve in his body" the fact was that he was

*In the early days of the Alaska Bush pilot, any flat stretch of land could be – and usually was – used as a landing strip. In Valdez, the mud flats were an excellent place to land as long as you could get the plane off the flats before the tide came in. Here, in 1938, Bob Reeve is caught in what was called "Mudville" with his cargo above the high tide line but not into the car yet.* Photo Courtesy of the University of Alaska Anchorage Archives.

doing more than flying by instinct. While most pilots flew by following dog trails in the snow or by using a pocket compass and a crude map, Gillam was a technology freak. Early in his career he established a network of radio stations on the ground in the areas where he flew and trusted friends flicked them on whenever they knew Gillam was in the area. He also studied meteorology and weather maps and stayed current on the state-of-the-art in navigational aides. He installed and used a directional gyro, altimeter, direction-finder and other navigational tools which, in the late 1930s, were considered more magician's tricks than aviation mainstays. Gillam was adept at using his tools and that was what kept him alive.

With all of the jokes and antics aside, death was a pilot's constant companion. "You don't have to go up," the old saying goes, "but you do have to come down" and every pilot knew that whenever he went up, he might not have a choice of where, when or how he was going to come down.

When Fred Chambers was missing on the Nulato River in January of 1939, Hans Mirow and a score of other pilots went out looking for him. On the first day, Mirow was caught in a whiteout while following a wide swath cut in the forest for a telegraph wire. Mirow nicked some trees about eight miles from Kaltag and came down hard. It took rescuers several days to find his body. That was the price of flying in the North.

Sometimes the living paid just as high a price. In February of 1940, CAA pilot Benton W. Steve Davis went down outside of Cordova. He survived the crash but discovered that his foot was wedged beneath a panel. For the next 24 hours he sat helplessly as his foot froze. Finally he was able to retrieve his pistol and shoot his foot free. He lived, but it took some time in the hospital for him to recover.[13]

The Golden Age of the bush pilot was an era of few regulations. The pilots flew as they wanted, charged what they could get away with and thumbed their noses at the authorities. It was a wild and woolly era, and they, the Bush Pilots, were the cowboys of the skies. Then came the CAA with its rules and regulations. Four years later, the world of the Alaska bush pilot was turned upside down.

*Wind, rain and snow were not the only problems that the Alaska Bush pilot had to face. There were also volcanoes which would erupt with little notice. This is the eruption of Mt. Veniaminof in March of 1944. At one time the volcano was 20,000 feet, almost as tall as Mt. McKinley before it 'blew its top off.' The black smoke is very dangerous to airplanes because the thick ash can clog aircraft engines.* Courtesy of the University of Alaska Fairbanks, Rasmuson Library.

Chapter 6

# THE THOUSAND MILE WAR

THE SECOND WORLD WAR BROUGHT UNEXPECTED CHANGES to Alaska, even before the attack on Pearl Harbor. In March of 1941, the United States military decided to open an air corridor to Siberia. The USSR and Great Britain were fighting Adolf Hitler's Germany and they needed American equipment and supplies, particularly airplanes. At that point, America was neutral and wanted to remain that way, but also wanted to help its traditional friend, Great Britain, and her allies. The United States resolved the problem of "staying neutral" by designing a political program known as Lend-Lease. While the United States would remain officially neutral, it would lend or lease aircraft and supplies to Britain and the Soviet Union, who would pay for the usage or loss after the war. Planes on their way to England went via the East Coast while aircraft on their way to Russia went through Alaska. But American pilots could not fly the planes out of the United States. So they would fly them to Alaska and turn them over to the Soviet crews which would then fly them out of the country.

Prior to the Alaska-Siberia Route, (ALSIB), planes flown to the Soviet Union were traveling through the Middle East and putting 13,000 miles on the aircraft before the planes ever saw combat. The ALSIB cut that distance to 3,000 miles. From September, 1942, until the end of the war, Soviet crews received almost 8,000 fighters and bombers in Fairbanks, flew them to a small air field 100 miles north of Nome, named Port Clarence, and then across the Bering Sea to Siberia.

Once the United States was dragged into the Second World War, Americans no longer had to pretend to be neutral and that ended lend lease. But it did not end Alaska's role as a front line of the war. While every American history buff knows that the Japanese staged a surprise attack on Pearl Harbor in the Hawaiian Islands on December 7, 1941, few remember that the Japanese also bombed Alaska and actually landed on and controlled two islands in the Aleutian chain.

On June 3 and 4, 1942, two Japanese aircraft carriers with 82 planes—protected by two heavy cruisers and three destroyers—launched a surprise air raid on Dutch Harbor in the Aleutians. An American PBY Catalina had spotted the invasion fleet before it actually arrived at Dutch Harbor so it was not truly a surprise attack, but the damage was substantial nonetheless.

After the initial bombing, the Japanese seized two of the last islands in the Aleutians, Attu and Kiska. This was the first time invaders had occupied American soil since the War of 1812. This was just as good for morale in Japan as it was bad news in the United States.

Attu and Kiska were key to the Japanese control of the air space over the Pacific Ocean. With long range airplanes based in Attu and Kiska, the Japanese Air Force could strike to the east at American forces in Alaska or attack American convoys crossing the Pacific to the south. Long range Japanese fighter planes from the island of Midway could control all the area of the Pacific which the planes from Attu and Kiska could not reach.

But there was one problem in this sequence of logic. The Battle of Midway, which took place a few days after the bombing of Dutch Harbor, was a disaster for the Japanese. They lost four aircraft carriers, 275 airplanes and more than 4,800 men. On a global scale, the Japanese lost the southern footing for their grand plan to control the airspace over the Pacific. Their failure to take Midway effectively left the Japanese soldiers on Attu and

Kiska with no mission to fulfill. But the troops remained on the island, primarily as a morale booster for the Japanese public and only secondarily as a fighting force that could be used to attack any allied invasion fleet steaming across the Pacific.

Fortunately for Alaska, the invasion of the Japanese brought new meaning to the term North to Alaska. Overnight, the United States military became aware of the danger of leaving an exposed northern flank and the Pentagon began to pour

*The United States Army Air Corp – which would become the United States Air Force – bombed the island of Kiska heavily before invasion forces were landed. When the invasion force hit the beach it discovered that the Japanese had fled the island.* Photo courtesy of the United States Air Force.

millions of dollars of supplies and equipment into the northland. The Japanese had to be contained on the islands they occupied and, eventually, they had to be driven out. But that would take men and supplies.

The first problem to be faced was as old as Alaska—lack of transportation corridors. There was no road to Alaska, air cargo routes were circuitous, barge traffic was slow, and weather stalled traffic on land, water and in the air for weeks at a time. The only reasonable method to move millions of tons of supplies into Alaska quickly was over land so a road had to be built. In a little over nine months, under summer and winter conditions so severe that any other project would have stalled, the United States Army constructed the Alaska-Canada Highway, immediately known as the Al-Can and today as the Alaska Highway.

At the same time, supplies were pouring in by ship to the now-rebuilt Dutch Harbor at the rate of 400,000 pounds a

*In what turned out to be some of the heaviest fighting during the Second World War, American solider disembarked on the rugged Aleutian shore. These troops are on Attu, the last island in the Aleutian Islands. One in four of these men would be killed or wounded as a result of combat here.* Photo courtesy of the United States Army.

month. Thus began the air war dubbed the Thousand Mile War, the distance referring to the length of the Aleutian chain of islands. With the Japanese flying east from their bases on Attu and Kiska and the Americans west from their supply bases in Kodiak and Dutch Harbor, the islands between Dutch Harbor and Attu were soon littered with the remains of Zeros, P-38s, B-25s, Aeoro-cobras, and Catalinas.

What neither side knew before the invasion but learned quickly was that the Aleutians were probably the worst place in the world to do battle. The islands were isolated from both Japan and North America by great distances across the turbulent North Pacific. Keeping men fed and equipment in top shape required a constant stream of cargo ships which were easy targets for the marauding airplanes of the other side. The Japanese on Kiska were taking such a heavy pounding from American bombers that the Japanese feared for their supply ships. As a result, they only shipped supplies for Kiska as far as Attu. From there the supplies were flown to Kiska.

The weather was another problem. Because the Aleutians divide the North Pacific from the Bering Sea, the islands are subject of violent storms when weather systems from the two oceans collide. As a result, the weather in the Aleutians is notoriously unpredictable. It can go from a dead calm to a howling storm in a matter of minutes. It was the only place in the world, pilots swore, where it was possible to have fog and a 50 mph wind at the same time. The wind could shift suddenly, or there could be two winds blowing in opposite directions immediately next to each other, or there could be no wind at all until a plane took off and then a 100 mph wind would come out of nowhere. It was not unusual for a plane to crab left against the wind as it began its takeoff and then be forced to crab right halfway down the runway because there were two strong winds blowing in opposite directions across the runway. Other times pilots reported wind socks that showed the wind blasting east at one end of the runway, west at the other end of the runway and a dead calm in the middle. Sometimes the pilots had to fight headwinds that were so strong that it would take them six hours to reach their destination. Then, on the return trip with a tail wind, they could cover the same distance in two hours.[14] The sudden, violent wind in the Aleutians was even given a special name, williwaw, and pilots quickly learned that flying in the Aleutians took a special skill—the ability to expect the unexpected.

Jokes about the weather—and particularly the cloud cover were common. As more than one pilot said, you knew the cloud cover was too thick for flying "if you can't see your co-pilot." You could test for altitude in the fog by sticking your hand out the window. "If it touches a ship's mast," the saying went, "you're flying too low." One pilot lost in fog claimed to have followed a duck to safety because he knew that a duck would

*Marston Matting.* Photo courtesy of the author.

not fly into a mountain. Another pilot flying a PBY that was fighting the wind claimed that a seagull landed on his wing. If the weather was too thick for a seagull, it was too dangerous for a PBY to be in the air so the pilot set the plane down on the water. There the seagull jumped off his wing—and swam away.

While Alaska winters are legendary for their length and deep cold, the winter of 1942-43 was exceptionally harsh. Temperatures in the Alaska Interior dropped to 67 below zero and, along the Aleutians, it was so cold that blow torches had to be used to warm airplane engines so they would start. It took hours to chip the ice off the planes. When the men weren't out in the cold working on the airplanes, they were shivering in their tents where temperatures didn't rise above freezing for weeks at a time.

The Aleutian soil was another problem. Because the islands were part of the so-called Ring of Fire, the ring of volcanic activity around the Pacific Rim, much of the earth was dark brown or black and covered with a form of tundra known as muskeg. With men and equipment moving on the muskeg, it turned to a muddy soup. Many times the men building roads or air strips were up to their knees in muck and when planes landed, they sent up rooster sprays of mud that obscured the vision of landing crews. On the ground or in the air, the Aleutian war was extremely trying for the pilots. If they weren't being buffeted by the winds in the air, they were flying through cloud cover hoping they were on course, or landing in mud that was ankle deep.

To defeat the Japanese in the Aleutians, the United States had to employ the same maneuvers as those being used in the South Pacific. The United States Army Air Corps —there was no United States Air Force yet—would take an island, build an airfield and then use that landing strip to take the next strategic location.

While the United States military could not solve the problem of the miserable weather, it did make the landing strips more functional by bringing in what was called Marston Matting. So-named because it was tested in Marston, North Carolina, each piece of matting looked like a ten-foot-long, 15-inch-wide piece of Swiss cheese. There were slots and hooks on the sides of each mat so that it could be attached to its neighbor. In this way, mat by mat, an entire landing strip could be constructed.

But it took a lot of the matting to make a runway. To cover a landing strip 5,000 feet long and 150 wide, it took 60,000 sheets of matting, a few dozen sledge hammers, and quite a few infantry men with raw hands and bruised knuckles. The mats could not just be laid out on the muskeg. The earth had to be leveled, which generated quite a bit of mud.

Though the mats provided the planes with a landing surface

more solid than mud, there was still more than enough mud to go around during the wet season. Whenever a plane touched down, it was usually followed by a spray of mud. Sometimes loose pieces of matting would snap free of the landing field and dance about before rolling to a stop. Other times the matting would undulate from the weight of the incoming plane like an ocean wave.

For many of the American pilots trained in the Lower 48, Alaska generally and the Aleutians particularly, the conditions were unexpectedly grim and while they had faith in their own fighters, they marveled that the Alaska bush planes could stay aloft. "Spare parts flying in formation," one of the Alaska bush pilots said lovingly of his plane. But the Army pilots quickly grew to respect these planes which often landed by "cracking up easy." These Alaska planes, the Army pilots noted, "had nine lives—like a cat." But the humor aside, they respected the planes because they performed. "The more I see the bush pilots fly, the less I fear an airplane" was an expression more than one military pilot in the Aleutians came to regard as a true statement.[15]

Even though the Japanese were only on two islands at the end of the Aleutians, Alaskans were on a war footing all across the territory. Everyone was jumpy. Bob Reeve was almost shot down when he flew into Juneau unannounced. When asked why he had not called ahead, Reeve reportedly snapped, "I would have circled around so you could see me but this happens to be an airplane, not a balloon, and I was out of gas and had to come down."[16] Even though he had a radio, Reeve rarely used it. "What do I want with a radio" he supposedly asked the CAA. "I have enough troubles of my own without fooling with a gadget like that." You have to have a radio because it's required, he was told. So Reeve had a radio—but he refused to use it for months.[17]

On the other hand, Archie Ferguson loved his radio. He'd talk to anyone anytime anywhere. Even when it was restricted. One of the best known incidents of Archie's career occurred during the Second World War when Archie was babbling into his microphone. The radio operator at Nome came on the air and advised Archie that only authorized chatter was allowed on the radio with one exception, an emergency.

"Cessna Two Zero Seven Six Six, do you declare this an emergency?" the radio operator asked.

"Yer darn right. Any time I'm in the air it's an emergency!"

But there were still the day-to-day risks of being a bush pilots and the close scrapes are legendary. Flying from Cold Bay in the Aleutians to Anchorage in the middle of the War, Bob Reeve encountered an ice storm and soon found that his plane was flying like a "hay barn." He had no de-icing equipment

*Robert "Bob" Reeve on the left.* Photo courtesy of the Reeve family.

and couldn't land because it was pitch dark. So he kept flying. Eventually the icing became so bad he could not see through his windshield so he opened the side window and navigated along the beach line of Cook Inlet. By the time he reached Anchorage he was only 200 feet off the ground and his prop was barely turning because of the ice. When he finally touched down, the CAA Inspector, Burleigh Putnam, shook his head sadly and said he didn't think it would have been possible for a plane with that much ice to stay aloft and then began lecturing

Reeve on flying in ice storms. "I get your point," Reeve told Putnam, "But I didn't pick up that ice on purpose."[18]

Gradually the American forces worked their way along the Aleutian Islands, island by island, toward Attu. Finally, the war in the Aleutians changed from an air war to a ground confrontation. On May 11, 1943, American troops hit the beaches at Attu at three points and pinched the Japanese into a valley. The fighting was fierce with the melting muskeg a

*During the Second World War the easiest home to build was called a Quonset. It could be put up quickly, defied the snow to build up on its roof and had not central ceiling beam. This meant the longest piece of wood in the building was about three feet long. This made it easy to transport all parts of the Quonset in a bush plane.* Photo courtesy of the Anchorage Museum Rasmuson Center.

hazard to both Japanese and American soldiers. After several weeks of shelling and firing, there were only 28 Japanese left alive from a contingent of 2,600. (On a per capita basis, Attu ranks as the second most costly American battle in terms of lives lost in the Pacific Theater.)

The victory at Attu was not the end of the war in the Aleutians. The United States invaded Kiska as well, only to discover that the Japanese had evacuated their men under cloud cover. Now, with the Aleutians clear of Japanese, American bombers could use the strategic airfields of Attu to bomb the Kurile

Islands and strategic targets on the island of Japan—including Tokyo. Ironically, the Aleutians began the war as a strategic card in the hands of the Japanese and ended up as a critical bombing base for the Americans.

But even though Alaska was a strategic location, it seemed that only the military took Alaska's pilots seriously. The banks certainly did not. Midway through the Second War, Bob Reeve was stranded in Seattle because he didn't have enough money to buy gas to fly back to Alaska. Reeve only knew one man who might help, Fowler Martin of the Pacific National Bank. At first blush, any loan was impossible. Reeve had no assets in Seattle to give the bank as security and Pacific National Bank had a strict policy of not loaning to bush pilots. But Martin knew Reeve personally and advanced the money anyway—which did not make Martin popular with his bank. Reeve was able to repay the loan in a year but often chuckled that during that year Martin "never picked up a daily paper without scanning the headlines to see whether I had crashed." Reeve didn't thus proving that, in Reeve's words, "the airplane was here to stay."[19]

The end of the war as a blessing as well. While the rest of the country was returning to peace time activities, Alaska received an sizable increase in military spending. The Pentagon had realized the strategic importance of Alaska, and, with the advance of technology, Alaska became a crucial part in the defense of the United States.

*Even after the Second World War, Alaska's landing strips were primitive. Here a Northern Consolidated aircraft offloads into an Army surplus vehicle. Note the river boat in the right background. Planes and boats often had to 'share' the riverbank.* Courtesy of the University of Alaska Fairbanks, Rasmuson Library.

Chapter 7

# POST-WAR ALASKA

THE END OF THE SECOND WORLD WAR BROUGHT A BOOM
of technology to the aviation industry generally, and an economic boom to Alaska specifically. By the 1950s, the United
States military had developed the ICBM, the inter-continental ballistic missile. During the Cold War—that time during
which the United States and Soviet Union appeared to be on
the brink of a nuclear war at any moment, roughly starting in
1948 and ending in the 1960s—one of the great fears of the
American military was that the Soviets would fire a missile that
could reach the United States half way around the world.

In those days, before the era of the geo-stationary satellite
and downward-looking radar, the United States military feared
that it would not know when an ICBM had been fired until
it was, quite literally, in American airspace. What they needed
was more time to react to the incoming ICBMs so that anti-
ICBM missiles could be sent aloft in time to shoot down the
incoming ICBM before any damage was done.

The only way to have more time was to detect the incoming ICBMs earlier. By placing radar bases as close to the Soviet Union as possible, the military would get the maximum
amount of warning time. Thus, in the mid-1950s, a string of
Distant Early Warning (DEW) sites were installed along the
coast of the Arctic Ocean. These stations would be the first to

give the alarm if an incoming ICBM suddenly appeared over the horizon.

As a backup to the DEW line sites, there was a string of NORAD, North American Air Defense, sites as well. Also built in the 1950s, these ran throughout the Alaska Interior and across Canada and, like the DEW line sites, were equipped with radars. If the DEW sites were knocked out, the NORAD would continue to broadcast the warning to the military bases in the Lower 48 and, secondarily, the NORAD sites were to watch the skies for incoming Soviet bombers and fighters. Once Soviet planes were spotted on the radar screen the NORAD sites would inform the American fighter aircraft at Elmendorf Air Force Base in Anchorage and Eielson Air Force Base in Fairbanks.

The oceans had to be watched as well. The Soviet Navy prowled the Bering Sea and the Soviet Air Force kept a sharp lookout for any aircraft that penetrated within 200 miles of the Soviet coast, what the USSR claimed as its territorial waters. Navigation by air was difficult because maps were only helpful near the coast. The dependable navigation system that was needed was provided by the United States Coast Guard in the form of LORAN, Long Range Aid to Navigation. A string of LORAN stations stretched from Southeast Alaska to Port Clarence, each station broadcasting at a different frequency so that planes could triangulate their exact position on a map. Any plane with a piece of LORAN equipment would pick up the signals from three LORAN stations. Since these stations were at different points of the compass, the LORAN equipment could figure out where the plane was by the angle at which the three beams were converging. This was then translated into longitude and latitude and the pilot could pinpoint his position on a map.

But in the 1960s the LORAN equipment was so expensive that most pilots could not afford the aid. As a result, they flew as they always had, by the seat of their pants. This led to quite a bit of danger with the polar bear hunts. Since the polar bears were found out on the ice pack, often hundreds of miles form shore, American bush pilots often strayed into Soviet airspace. In most cases the Soviets weren't that interested in the small planes flying over the ice pack, but when those planes actually landed in Siberia, they were very concerned. Then the Soviet Air Force would send their fighters aloft and harass every small plane they came across, flying so close to the small planes that the turbulence caused by the Soviet's jet engines would force the smaller planes down, sometimes to crash on the ice.

The United States Air Force took a very dim view of the Soviets penetrating American air space, and as soon as the incoming Soviet aircraft was picked up on American radar, American jets scrambled and went aloft. When an American aircraft met a Soviet fighter there was a courteous exchange of photos and waving. Then the Soviets were escorted back to their air space. These confrontations between Soviet and American war planes, known as intercepts, were frequent. This was understandable considering that United States claimed a 200 mile territorial limit when the distance between the Soviet Union and the United States was only a few hundred yards between the Diomede Islands and barely 15 miles between the closest point of the two mainlands—with Soviet and American radar bases within eyesight of one another.

But there was still one important missing piece to the military puzzle in Alaska: communication. Because geo-stationary satellite communication was still in the experimental stage, the bulk of the communication in the 1950s was done by was done by microwave or what was known as tropospheric scatter. Combined, this system, constructed by the United States military was known as White Alice.

With regard to microwave, wires were not required but signals could only go between two points which were line-of-sight. In other words, microwave transmissions went in a straight line. They could not be sent over a 100 mile distance because the curvature of the earth would have blocked the transmission. To solve this problem, huge transmission centers and smaller repeater stations were built all over Alaska. From Barrow to Ketchikan and Attu to the Canadian border, whenever an Alaskan picked up a phone, his or her voice was converted into a microwave and bounced from transmission station to repeater to repeater to repeater all across the Territory.

However, there were some parts of Alaska where it was not possible to place microwave towers or repeaters, like the Aleu-

*This is a White Alice site. It is one of a chain of microwave towers provided the communications backbone for the United States military in the Alaskan bush.* Photo courtesy of the United States Air Force.

tians. In these areas communication beams were bounced off the troposphere from one station to the next. The troposphere, that portion of atmosphere which lies from seven to 10 miles above the earth, acted much the same way as a backboard when a basketball is tossed against it. The radio beams, like the basketball, bounced. Sometimes these signals could be bounced as far as 200 miles.

These new technologies had a huge impact on Alaska. Every DEW, NORAD, LORAN and White Alice station had to be built. The bulk of the building material could be shipped north by barge but tons of it came in by plane. Carpenters and electricians were flown to the work site, and then had to be sup-

*Overloading a plane or loading it incorrectly has always been dangerous. Here you can see the consequences of putting too much weight in the back of plane.* Photo courtesy of the Anchorage Museum Rasmuson Center.

plied with food and medical supplies. Mail had to be delivered. Everything from nails to a roll of toilet paper, had to come by air. Before the Second World War, the bush pilots of Alaska struggled to survive on passenger service; after the War, their businesses boomed on cargo hauling. Solitary pilots formed airlines and small airline companies, like Alaska Airlines, got much bigger.

The sudden influx of construction put money in Alaskan pockets and the impact of those dollars was unmistakable. Alaskans could now travel more frequently and more money went into the airlines. With more money, Alaskans bought more goods from the Lower 48, which had to be transported back to Alaska by plane. Dollars were turning over faster and the airlines were booming.

To the present day, the impact of the Second World War can still be felt in remote parts of Alaska. All of the old landing strips are still being used, some for more than just emergencies. Those buildings that are still standing are used as shelters by hunters and downed pilots and Alaska's bush pilots still make a living flying mail, cargo, and passengers to the NORAD and LORAN sites that are still operating. (DEW and White Alice sites no longer exist.)

For the Alaska bush pilot, the Second World War and the Cold War could not have come at a better time. Just when it looked as though the bush pilot was going the way of the passenger pigeon, the war gave the bush pilot a new lease on life, a lease that continues to the present day.

But still there were problems. Equipment could not solve all the problems. Sam Shafsky, long-time bush pilot who flew for Archie, remembered a flight from Ruby, up the Yukon around Tanana and then into Fairbanks in the mid-1950s. The weather had been pretty good when he started but between Tanana and Manly Hot Springs clouds moved in, forcing him to fly lower and lower until he was skimming along inside a canyon a few hundred feet off the riverbank with mountain on each side.

"I could see something dark coming up so I pulled over a little bit and kept looked and saying to myself, 'What the Hell is that?'"

With each passing second, the object became darker. Then, in the last instant before it snapped into focus he realized it was another airplane, flying down the same canyon directly at him! The two planes were so close that neither could change course. Fortunately they were just far enough apart to whip by one another on opposite sides of the narrow canyon.

"I looked out the wind and saw it was Jimmy Stewart in a Pilgrim on the mail run from Fairbanks to Nulato! I looked at him and he looked at me (as if to say) what the Hell are you doing here?"

This era also highlighted many pilots of note whose experience added to the tales of Alaska. Veteran bush pilot Tony Schultz, who spent more than forty years flying the Alaskan bush, was as famous for his willingness to fly corpses and convicts as he was for his missions of mercy. Sometimes his antics were legendary. In the 1950s, for instance, he was chartered by the United States Marshal to pick up a man who was accused of killing his wife. Upon arrival in Chevak, Schultz learned that there had been a witness to the violent act who was also expecting to be flown back to Fairbanks. Besides Tony and the Marshal, this meant there was the husband, a witness against the husband and the corpse of the wife. This made five individuals to be flown in a plane with only four seats. Schultz, a veteran at hauling cargo in the bush, was unperturbed. He put the witness on the husband's lap and then strapped both of them into a back seat with same seat belt. That was the way things were done in the bush. After all, this was Alaska and people did things differently in the Northland.

*In Alaska, all modes of transportation mix. Here at Ladd Field in Fairbanks, a dog sled mushes past a C-47 Skytrain left and a C-46 Commando. When this picture was taken, 1944, the C-46 was the largest two-motor transport plane in the world. The dog sled could seat one uncomfortably.* Courtesy of the University of Alaska Fairbanks, Rasmuson Library.

Chapter 8

# THE TOURISM BOOM

THEN CAME AN EVEN GREATER BOOM. DURING THE 1950S, Americans in the Lower 48 were suddenly flush. The GI Bill allowed hundreds of thousands of American soldiers to go to college. By the mid-1950s, they were reaping the rewards of a college education. These now-affluent Americans were traveling, and high on their list of domestic destinations was the Land of the Midnight Sun.

Into the early 1960s, there were two traditional tours of Alaska. One was on the cruise lines following the Inside Passage along the coast of British Columbia and Alaska. This duplicated the route of Alaska's Gold Rush stampeders at the close of the previous century. The largest line was Princess, a company still in business today, which started in Vancouver, B. C. and went as far north as Skagway or Haines at the top of the Lynn Canal. This was a luxury cruise with stopovers in Southeastern Alaskan cities such as Ketchikan and Juneau.

The other traditional tour began with a flight into Anchorage. From there the travelers could go south to fish for king salmon and halibut on the Kenai Peninsula. Or they could go north by train, passing through McKinley National Park on their way to Fairbanks. After a stay in Fairbanks, the tourists often flew back to Anchorage and then the Lower 48.

But with the boom in the tourism industry, and more and

more Americans looking for the real Alaska, tour companies sprang up in communities such as Nome, Bethel, Barrow, Kotzebue and Unalakleet. Hotels and restaurants appeared in communities that had never seen a need for such establishments. Local convention and visitors bureaus were formed to lure tourists to exotic locations where they could see Eskimo blanket tosses, take nature tours along the Arctic Ocean, and embark upon photographic safaris on the tundra in the north or in the rain forests of the south. Small and large, the tour companies capitalized on the mystic of Alaska, its unique animals and stunning settings. Alaska Airlines even went so far as to paint the face of an Eskimo on the side of its planes to symbolize its roots in the northland, a feature that continues to this day.

Many of the pilots were not above making a tourism boom of their own. One October in the mid-1950s, an innkeeper in Fort Yukon by the name of Gilbert Lord, devised a clever scheme to keep his hotel full during the fall. Procuring a vial of gold, he showed it to anyone who came through Fort Yukon and swore this gold had come from the bottom of a fish wheel. No one seemed to question that Lord might have an ulterior motive in wanting an influx of people in an area where he had the only hotel, and it did not take long for the word to leak out. In Fairbanks, 100 miles away, there was a general infection of the gold bug aided by the *Fairbanks Daily News Miner* and the radio station.

All you needed was a pick, shovel, pan and a "pack sack full of grub," remembered Fairbanks bush pilot Jim McGoffin, who was long accused of actually precipitating the strike. McGoffin, a bush pilot, also had every reason to be supportive of the strike. This was, after all, probably the first stampede in world history where the gold rushers were airlifted to the diggings. At the peak of the epidemic of gold fever, McGoffin was making four trips a day to Fort Yukon and "hardly made a dent in the line of people waiting impatiently to board our next flight."

Bill Lavery, another bush pilot out of Fairbanks, true to the spirit of gold stampedes on the Last Frontier, found a more lucrative cargo. He was air lifting beer, 3,000 pounds of it on his first trip. This was 1,000 pounds over the legal load limit for his Norseman but the profit motive was strong. His plane was so overloaded that he could not make it over the mountains to Fort Yukon so he had to fly up the southern flowing watershed to its confluence with the Yukon and then up the Yukon River to the Native village.

*Tourism, particularly hunting, became big business for Alaska's bush pilots in the 1950s. Alaska has some of the largest bears in the world and hunting for brown bear in Alaska was a safari in itself.* **Photo courtesy of Anchorage Museum Rasmuson Center.**

Lavery wasn't the only one trying to "get it while you can." Fairbanks merchants had set up tents all along the river in hopes of making a killing on the impending boom. Girls were available as companions and booze flowed freely. It was a boomtown with all of the activities that are normally associated with a strike.

*This is a typical landing strip in the bush during the winter. There are no amenities, just a place to land. You can see the snow plow in the lower left portion of the photograph.* Photo courtesy of the author.

But it only lasted about a week. When no one found any gold, the would-be stampeders, many of them suffering from

acute cases of bourbon flu, returned to Fairbanks. Then the air traffic reversed itself. That ended what was known in the Interior as the Great Fish Wheel Gold Strike.

Jim McGoffin pleaded "Not Guilty" to instigating the strike. But, as he had clearly profited from the momentary insanity, he also added "I sure didn't do anything to stop it."[20]

*A cow with other cargo being transported to the Bush.* Photo courtesy of the Anchorage Museum Rasmuson Center.

As an interesting aside, many of the pilots of Alaska also saw the end of the Second World War as an unexpected bonanza for aviation. As fast as the military abandoned its air bases, the pilots were there to salvage what equipment and supplies they could find. From one end of the Territory to the other, Marston Matting disappeared by the mile. No sooner were the military personnel gone than pilots would swoop down on the airfields, fill their planes with the sheets of the matting and fly them back to their local landing strip where the matting would be re-assembled. Anything that wasn't nailed down disappeared, and then reappeared on local landing strips.

Perhaps the greatest scavenger of all was Archie Ferguson. Archie wasn't satisfied with absconding with everything that wasn't nailed down; he went after everything whether it was nailed down or not. One summer after the war he arrived at

*Not all cargo can fit comfortably into a bush plane.* Photo courtesy of the Anchorage Museum Rasmuson Center.

the abandoned military air strip of Port Clarence with his barge and proceeded to steal buildings—as many as 30 of them. He took them apart like so many modular homes, stacked them on his barge and returned to Kotzebue. Some are still standing in Kotzebue today.

The end of the Second World War brought a boom in Alaska big game hunting similar to the African safaris of the last century. Not only did Alaska have brown bears that tipped the scales at 1,200 pounds, there were also grizzly, moose, Dall sheep and musk ox. But the animal that drew hunters north, and specifically to the Arctic, was the polar bear.

Beginning in the mid-1950s and ending with the passage of the Marine Mammals Protection Act of 1972, Alaska's Arctic turned into a hunter's paradise for polar bear weighing more than half a ton and providing a skin large enough to cover a living room floor. But hunting polar bear was very dangerous. The only time to hunt the bears was when the Bering Sea had a mantle of ice three feet thick. This allowed the bears to roam on the ice pack looking for food as far south as Kotzebue.

Once ice formed on the sea, hunters boarded small planes and headed out over the ice pack. They would fly for hours, looking for tracks. When they saw tracks, they would follow them until they found the bear. Landing well ahead of the animal, the hunters would set up an ambush. Then, as the bear approached, they would shoot it. The airplanes didn't bother the bears—the polar bear was the largest animal on the ice and feared nothing.

Hunting this way sounds easy. It was not. The temperature averaged 20 below zero on the ice pack. If anything went wrong, like a airplane engine freezing up, the hunter and pilot might freeze to death before they could be found. It was also cold enough that guns could easily jam. Being on the ice with a jammed gun as a half-ton, meat-eating animal armed with six inch teeth charged was not a circumstance many hunters favored. Polar bears had no fear of men or airplanes which meant that if the bear were wounded and not killed, there was no telling what might happen. In the mid-1960s, Ken Oldham, a polar bear guide with a decade of seasons in the Arctic, once watched a wounded polar bear attack his running plane engine.

Thinking about shooting a polar bear while sitting in a comfortable room in Ohio is a bit different than actually standing behind a block of ice in temperatures ranging down to 50 below zero and watching an animal the size of a bulldozer coming straight at you. The first time Archie Ferguson went after polar bear he went with a seasoned hunter, an Eskimo by the name of Herman Ticket. They set their ambush but as soon as the bear approached, Archie lost his nerve and broke for the airplane. Clambering aboard he started the engine and made for the sky.

Ticket, not wanting to be left alone on the ice with the polar bear, dashed after Archie. But he was wasn't quick enough to make it inside the plane. The best that he could do was step on a ski. As Archie went aloft, Ticket was on the plane's ski holding onto a strut for dear life.

In addition to all of the problems on the ice, flying conditions were hazardous. At that time of year the sun was only up for a few hours each day, and every pilot had to make the most of the daylight. Planes were in the air no earlier than 9 am and had to be back by three in the afternoon. The rest of the time it was pitch black. In addition, the ice on the surface of the Bering Sea was not flat and smooth. There were ice hills and depressions, pressure ridges and even open water stretches, called polynyas, as well as ice blocks as large as a house whose size could not be detected from the air. This made landing on the ice so hazardous that it did not take long for the polar bear hunters to learn to travel in pairs. One plane took the client and the second was packed to the windows with extra fuel, survival gear and food.

But the flying conditions in the Arctic were still pitiless and the bush pilot had to resourceful to stay alive. Nelson Dinky Walker was flying over Kotzebue one winter in the 1960s when he realized that one of his skis was hanging free. It had slipped free of its latching device and Walker could not land safely with the ski in that position. Thinking quickly, he radioed an Eskimo, Tommy Sours, on the ground for assistance. Sours found an old broom handle and a snow machine. Hurtling over the snow at the same speed as the airplane, Sours used the broom handle to maneuver the ski into position and then snap the ski in place.

Also in Kotzebue in the same era, Ken Oldham had difficulty with a ski. But his problem was that the ski had to be secured with pressure from on top of the ski. A friend on a snow machine matched his speed to that of the airplane and extended a broom handle to Oldham's hand outside the window of the Supercub. Once he had a grip on the pole, Oldham powered the plane into a steep bank. The moment gravity forced the ski to flop into place, Oldham planted the broom handle against the ski to secure it and then wedged the top of the broom pole against the underside of his wing. It held the ski in place long enough for him to land and manually attached the ski.

The polar bear hunting era in Alaska was short. It began in the late 1940s and ended in 1972 with the passage of the Marine Mammals Act. Although a polar bear is not technically a marine mammal, it was covered by the federal legislation and overnight the polar bear became a protected species. This brought to an end the polar bear trophy hunting business in the Arctic.

*This shot was taken of Star Airways float plane. Alaskans used to chuckle at the name because Star, backwards, spelled rats.* Courtesy of the University of Alaska Fairbanks, Rasmuson Library.

Chapter 9

# THE VIEW FROM THE TOP OF THE WORLD

THOUGH THE GOLDEN AGE OF THE BUSH PILOT PASSED with the Second World War, the Alaska bush pilot is not like the cowboy of the American West. The bush pilot still has a place in Alaska. About one-third of the residents of Alaska still live in the Bush and most villages do not have a runway long enough to accommodate a jet. As a result, small planes still fly passengers and cargo into and out of these communities. Whether it is a patient bound for a Fairbanks hospital, a drug counselor on her way to a conference in Anchorage, or a Native leader on his way to lobby the legislature in Juneau for a water treatment plant in his village, the trip starts in a bush plane.

But as Alaska has changed, so has the job of the bush pilot. So have the planes and instruments. In the days of Archie Ferguson and Mudhole Smith, a compass and a radio were the only pieces of navigational equipment in the cockpit. Today, most of the bush pilots have artificial horizons, VHF, Omnidirectional Range (VOR), altimeters, Distance Measuring Equipment (DME), Automatic Direction Finder (ADF), gyrocompasses, and often LORAN. Belly tanks extend the flying time of the aircraft and STOL (Short Take Off and Landing) kits can reduce the number of feet needed for landing and take-off on airstrips.

What this means in nuts-and-bolts terms is that a pilot can

now "see" through fog and storm clouds with radar and can land and take off from shorter air strips. He can pinpoint himself precisely on a map even if he is hundreds of miles from the nearest LORAN station and can fly for hours in darkness with his plane level and his course precisely set by a distant transmission tower. He can also land without the aid of lights or flare pots. Forty years ago, this technology was nothing more than a pilot's dream.

But many of the same problems faced by the bush pilots of the Golden Era are still present today. Even with the most sophisticated weather prediction equipment, planes and pilots still have to fly in the frigid weather. When Alaska experienced the lowest temperatures ever recorded on earth—with temperatures reaching 90 below zero in some cases—bush planes were in the air. Alaskans in remote villages were running out of fuel oil and someone had to get fuel and food into those villages. Rugged men and women bundled themselves into parkas, bunny boots and "fat boy" pants

*Even today, Alaska planes have special modifications for carrying cargo into the bush.*
Photo courtesy of Danny Daniels.

and flew. Day after day they flew—the lifeline to villages scattered across Alaska. These men and women made the difference between life and death to hundreds of Alaskans. No jet could do what these bush planes did.

But even with the advances in technology, the bush pilot still faces circumstances that are unique to Alaska. In the early 1980s, Anchorage bush pilot Jim O'Meara took off from Lime Village and learned first hand of the impact of physics on flying. It was

*Jim O'Meara.* Photo courtesy of Danny Daniels.

30 below zero on the runway but once he was 3,000 feet off the ground, the temperature rose to 40 degrees above zero. In a matter of minutes the temperature had jumped 70 degrees!

O'Meara appreciated the warmer temperatures but all the way into Anchorage he kept hearing a sweeping noise on the outside of his airplane. None of his instruments gave a clue as to what the sound was, and it was only when he landed that he learned what the strange noise had been. At 30 degrees below zero, every part of his plane was at the same temperature. Then, when he rose into the 40 above zero belt of air, the parts of plane warmed and expanded at different rates. The paint on the plane expanded faster than the fuselage so it bubbled and popped. Then the air rushing along the outer surfaces of the plane stripped the paint shreds off the plane. By the time O'Meara landed in Anchorage, he had lost all the paint on his aircraft.

And there is still human error. Today, many Alaska bush pilots make their living flying climbers to and from Mt. McKinley. Talkeetna, about 70 miles north of Anchorage, is a Mecca for mountain climbers and each year hundreds of men and women are flown up to the base camp from where they will climb to the summit. Bush pilots also provide search and rescue missions as well as air drop food to the climbing parties.

Doug Geeting, one of the best known mountain pilots in Talkeetna, learned a very important lesson concerning human error when he was air dropping food around Christmas in the mid-1980s. Usually Geeting flew with a cargo handler with whom he had worked before. For some reason he had to fly with a new cargo handler this trip, a young woman who didn't have that much experience with dropping cargo. Geeting packed his plane so he could make a number of drops. This meant stacking the cargo strategically so as he came to the first encampment of mountain climbers, he could eject the first load of food. There was no reason to attach parachutes to the cargo because all the supplies would hit was snow, a natural cushion.

As it happened, the first encampment wanted a 20-pound halibut. While this was a strange request for Christmas, it was no more unusual than other cargo Geeting had handled so he loaded it on board. Just before ground zero at the first encampment, the one which had requested the fish, Geeting turned to his cargo handler and yelled "Halibut!."

The cargo handler, unfamiliar with her task, thought Geeting had yelled "All of it!" and so she proceeded to dump all of the

cargo from the back of the plane out the open hatch. It was like a cascade of groceries falling from the sky and the supplies hit the camp with the effect of a bombing raid. The halibut obliterated a tent and a case of beer smashed through another, exploding on impact and spraying the two men inside. Other cargo peppered the encampment.

*Doug Geeting.* Photo courtesy of Danny Daniels.

Feeling the plane get unusually light, Geeting turned and to his horror saw that all the goods were gone. After the cargo handler explained that she thought he had said "All of it!" Geeting turned the plane around and headed back to the encampment to assess the damage. But as soon as he approached the camp, he could see people scattering in all directions. They thought he was coming back for a second run!

Bush pilots are still called upon to make unusual rescues. In the late 1970s, Jim O'Meara was asked to rescue a climber that was stuck on a precipice near the top of a mountain. Fighting a ferocious wind, he finally made it to where the climber was marooned. The man was huddled in a tent and when he heard O'Meara he crawled out. It was his lucky day. Facing his plane into the wind, O'Meara matched his air speed to the wind speed and then cut back on the throttle. Slowly the plane settled, coming down vertically. The plane's wheel hit the tent and in the next instant, the wind had stripped it off the mountain side. The climber reached up, grabbed the door handle and opened the door of the settling aircraft.

"Once I saw his knees (and knew both his legs were in the plane)," O'Meara said. "I was gone."

Sometimes the modern technology on the ground has led to improvements in flying conditions in the air. Alaskans love pizza just as much as other Americans. But some Alaskans live so far from a pizza parlor that the circular food has to be flown in. During the winter, many bush pilot have learned to put the sizzling pizza-to-go in plastic sacks to hold in the heat—and then place the sacks over their feet to keep them warm. Big Mac Attacks are not unknown in Alaska and sometimes the McDonald's in Juneau specifically receives an order for enough Big Macs to feed an entire city, which, sometimes, is exactly what is happening. Then bush planes arrive on their "errand of mercy" for there are many small communities in Alaska where McDonald's burgers are an import.

Though modern technology has made some of the functions of the bush pilots obsolete, it has opened the door to other opportunities. Through the 1960s and 1970s, for example, televisions in Alaska picked up local stations only. All programming was done on what was known as a tape delay. Programs were taped in Seattle and then flown to Anchorage and Fairbanks where they were re-broadcast. The taped evening news came on the same day, but other programs could be a week later—or longer. In some parts of Alaska it was not unusual to watch a Christmas Special in February.

Cable television has made the tape delay obsolete. Alaskans can now watch football games at the time they are actually played, enjoy CNN around the clock, or watch rock concerts

on MTV. Cable television has eliminated the need for bush pilots to fly television tapes into remote communities, but it has opened the door to video tapes for consumers. The bush pilots are still carrying tapes, it's just that the tapes these days are for video stores, not television stations.

*An ACWS (Air Craft Warning System) station. These stations monitor the skies over the Alaskan horizon to detect incoming Russian bombers.* Photo courtesy of the United States Air Force.

The advance in technology has helped pilots in others ways as well. One of the problems bush pilots used to face was how to adjust their schedule for the changeover from skis to pontoons. The change from pontoons to skis is not difficult as pilots simply pull their planes out of the water long enough for the ice to freeze. Even if it takes a few weeks before the change is made, the pilot can still land on ice with pontoons—though this is not a recommended practice. But when spring breaks the back of winter and the lakes and streams become ice free, a pilot cannot wait too long to make the change.

But in the spring, the changeover from skis to pontoons necessarily means that the pilot must come up with an alternate method of getting the plane back to the lake. One way is to place the plane with the pontoons on a flat trailer hooked to a pick up truck. Then, with the plane's engine running full throttle, the pickup races down the runway. When the proper airspeed is reached, the bush plane lifts off the trailer and flies away. But the trick is making sure you have reached the proper airspeed before the truck reaches the end of the landing strip.

With the opening of the Pacific Rim Alaska is finding itself, once again, in a strategic geographic position. By sea, it is days closer to Japan than Seattle and has two products Japan needs badly: fish and petroleum. Russia is also looking to Alaska for assistance. With the collapse of the Soviet Union, Russians in the Far East view Alaska as their cultural and economic partner. Both areas share the same weather, latitude, Native groups, and, most important, resources. Alaska businesses are now operating in Siberia and there are regular flights between Alaska and several Siberian cities. Siberian products are finding their way to the United States via Alaska and American products are being sold in Siberia by Alaskan entrepreneurs. But both regions still have the same difficulties with weather and transportation. The Bering Sea and Arctic Ocean are only ice free for three months each year. The rest of the year, everything that is needed to keep the industries operating has to be transported by plane.

The development of the petroleum industry on the shores of Prudhoe Bay on the Arctic Ocean created another boom for the Alaska bush pilot. Scientists knew there was oil in the Prudhoe Bay area, but it was not until the early 1970s that it was economically feasible to build the 800 mile pipeline. Today, more than one million barrels of oil a day flows from Prudhoe Bay to Valdez, about 18% of the United States' daily production. By comparison, enough petroleum comes down the TransAlaska Pipeline each day to satisfy all of California's energy needs for that day.

With the development of the oil industry on the shores of the Arctic Ocean, the Bush pilots had a new client. In Prudhoe Bay, Alaska, where the TransAlaska Pipeline starts, the work schedule is one-week-on-one-week-off. Men and women scheduled to work from Tuesday to Tuesday have to be flown in and out from Anchorage. Smaller planes move engineers, surveyors, and biologists all across the North Slope of the Brooks Range

*Today, Alaska's gold is black. It's oil and here are two welders work-ing in temperatures that will dip to 100 below zero with a wind chill.* Photo courtesy of Danny Daniels.

on oil-development related excursions. Press trips and tours of United States congressmen, congresswomen and foreign dig-nitaries also have to be done in smaller airplanes. Security on the TransAlaska Pipeline is handled by small airplanes, as is the search for oil leaks and other hazards that might damage the 800 mile conduit.

Small planes are also used for oil exploration and oil spill clean up because only a small plane can cover great distances and land on almost any surface. Whether landing on the tundra near an oil rig or near a oil-slickened beach, the most inexpensive and reasonable means of transportation is still the bush plane, as long as it is flown by experienced bush pilots.

The bush plane is also used by government and private-sector biologists for wildlife population counts and transporting animals from one region to another. Archie Ferguson may have had trouble with polar bear cubs, but today live, adult bears are tranquilized and flown to remote areas. The bears have not been known to wake up during the trip but their fitful sleep has made more than one pilot nervous.

The Russian Far East also offers unlimited opportunities for the bush pilot. Like Alaska, the Russian Far East is a land of scattered, small communities and a growing petroleum industry. Pilots are going to be needed to survey the land for pipelines as well as fly people out to hospitals and supplies into remote villages. The world may be changing, but in the Arctic regions, the ancient problems of weather and transportation still exist. And because of them, the Alaska bush pilot will continue to be a mainstay of the Alaska economy and American history well into the next century.

# SOURCE NOTES

1. Potter, Jean. *THE FLYING NORTH*. Macmillan, 1947, p. 145.

2. Fred Chambers interview with Steven C. Levi, Levi Papers, University of Alaska, Anchorage.

3. Jim Hutchison interview with Steven C. Levi, Levi Papers, University of Alaska, Anchorage.

4. Jacobson Interview with Steven C. Levi, Levi Papers, University of Alaska, Anchorage.

5. Beth Day, page 138.

6. Beth Day, page 86.

7. Beth Day, page 139.

8. Beth Day, page 141.

9. Fred Goodwin interview with Steven C. Levi, Levi Papers, University of Alaska, Anchorage.

10. Burleigh Putnam interview with Steven C. Levi, Levi Papers, University of Alaska, Anchorage.

11. Westover comments to Levi, February 8, 1994.

12. Cordova paper, August 8, 1941, in the scrapbook of Bertha Smith, Mudhole's Widow.

13. Cordova Paper, February 19, 1940, in the possession of Bertha Smith, Mudhole Smith's widow.

14. Garfield, page 135.

15. Chelnov, page 9.

16. Beth Day, page 181.

17. Potter, page 164.

18. Beth Day, page 214.

19. Beth Day, page 180.

20. McGoffin interview with Cliff Cernick, 1992, by permission of Jim McGoffin.

# GLOSSARY

**ADF**: Automatic Direction Finder, navigation equipment which allows a pilot to "lock onto" a radio frequency and follow the electronic beam.

**Al-Can**: the Alaska Canada Highway, now known as the Alaska Highway. Built at the start of the Second World War, the highway connected Alaska with the Lower 48. Originally a dirt and gravel road that turned to mud in the winter, it is not paved.

**Alaska Highway**: The current name for the Al-Can Highway.

**Aleut**: a Alaska Native.

**Aleutian Chain**: the chain of islands reaching westward from the Alaska mainland toward Siberia.

**Altimeters**: navigation equipment which shows how high plane is flying.

**Anti-ICBM missiles**: missiles which were designed to intercept incoming Inter-Continental Ballistic Missiles (ICBMs) and destroy them in the air before the ICBMs hit their designated targets.

**Artificial horizon**: navigation equipment which shows when the plane is flying level.

**Athabaskan**: the Athabaskan Indians live in Alaska's Interior. The three other Native groups include the Eskimo (Yupik, Siberian and Inupiat) Aleuts and Tlingit/Haida/Tsimshian Indians.

**Barabara**: the winter homes of the Eskimos of Alaska. Though they are sometimes called an igloo, the barabara is made of driftwood, sod and sometimes whale bone. Part of the structure is below ground. Alaska Eskimo do not live in snow and ice igloos.

**Belly tanks**: an auxiliary gas tank which is attached to the "belly" or bottom of a bush plane to give it extended range.

**Bunny boots**: oversized, white, rubber boots issued by the military that use air for insulation. They are called bunny boots because they are so oversized they appear as jack rabbit feet. Since the boots use air for insulation, a valve must be installed so that when they are used in an airplane the pressure in the boot can be released. Bush pilots have been known to surreptitiously twist the valve of a Cheechako's bunny boots closed so that when the plane rises several thousand feet, the Cheechako's feet are squeezed uncomfortably.

**Bush**: anyplace in Alaska that cannot be reached by a road that connects with the Lower 48. Approximately 1/3 of Alaska's population lives in the Bush.

**Bush pilot**: a pilot who makes his or her living flying cargo, passengers, supplies and animals into and out of the Bush.

**Bush plane**: a plane used in the Bush. Usually it means a plane that is unquestionably dependable. Sometimes it has added adaptations for used in the Bush, such as STOL, belly tanks, or tundra tires.

**Bypass mail:** a special class of mail in Alaska that allows a wider variety of items to be sent through the United States Postal Service.

**Call and wait:** how Bush residents make arrangements for a Bush plane. They call request for transportation and wait for a plane to arrive.

**Cheechako:** a tenderfoot or newcomer, someone who has not made a winter in Alaska from freeze-up to break-up. The term allegedly came about when a Skagway Native asked a new comer from where he had come. "Chicago," replied the tenderfoot. "Cheechako," replied the Native and the term stuck.

**Conservation:** the concept of preserving natural resources, vistas and resources for future generations.

**Crab:** to angle a plane to take advantage of the wind. If you go to a small airport on a windy day you will see planes landing that appear to be "coming in sideways." This is crabbing. If a strong wind is blowing across the runway, a pilot will turn his plane into the wind: or "crab": so that he can use the wind to slow his plane. On takeoff, the pilot would crab into the wind so he could increase the surface area of the wings that are exposed to the wind.

**DEW:** Distant Early Warning sites, a string of radar installations on the shore of the Arctic Ocean designed to detect incoming ICBMs from what was once the Soviet Union.

**DME:** Distance Measuring Equipment, navigation equipment that measures the distance between the airplane and the VOR station. (See VOR)

**Eskimo:** Natives who live along the coastlines of Alaska as far south as Bethel and as far north as St. Lawrence Island (Savoonga and Gambel).

**Fat boy pants:** thick, nylon, insulated pants originally issued by the military which are very warm but give the wearer the impression of being grossly overweight.

**Flare pots:** anything visible from the air during the day could be used to mark off a runway on the sea or river ice. At night flare pots were used. In the Golden Age of the Bush Pilot, flare pots could be as primitive as a coffee can – what coffee grounds came in before plastic bags for those born after 1970 – filled with diesel oil.

**Geo-stationary satellite:** a communications satellite which orbits the earth at the same rate of speed that the earth rotates. In essence, the satellite stays directly overhead and signals can be "bounced" to other satellites or earth stations.

**Gyrocompass:** a compass which are not affected by the planes motion or pitch. In other words, even if the plane is flying upside down, the gyrocompass can still be used.

**ICBM:** an Inter-Continental Ballistic Missile, a missile with a nuclear warhead that had such a long range that it could be fired at the United States from well inside the borders of the USSR and travel to the heartland of the United States.

**Icing:** Icing is the process where moisture in the air comes in contact with an airplane and turns to ice. An example would be a pilot flying at 5,000 feet where it is raining. When he drops to 3,000 feet he discovers that the temperature is below freezing. All of the rain that was his plane is now ice and freezing rain from the 5,000 foot level is coating his plane thicker and thicker and a sheet of ice is growing. This is very dangerous because ice adds weight to a plane. With each passing minute, the plane picks up weight. If it picks up too much weight, it will become too heavy to remain aloft and tumble out of the sky.

**Intercepts**: when fighters from the United States Air Force went aloft to stop Soviet airplanes from penetrating American air space.

**Kuspuk**: a summer parka, usually made of brightly colored fabric which Eskimo women traditionally wore as a summer covering. The winter, outer wear covering was called a parky and was constructed of fur with cotton batting. The kuspuk was utilitarian because it had a wide front pocket that ran across the front which could be filled with berries

**Line-of-sight**: microwaves, like a line-of-sight vision, can only go in a straight line from one visible target to the next.

**LORAN**: Long Range Aid to Navigation, the signal centers established by the United States Coast Guard which can be monitored by ships, boats and planes to triangulate their exact position on a map. LORAN is so accurate that 1,000 miles away from the LORAN station, the LORAN machine will be within 1,000 feet of precisely accurate.

**Lower 48**: the 48 contiguous states of the United States.

**Marston matting**: the Swiss cheese-like metal matting which was used as temporary landing fields. It was named Marston Matting because it was manufactured in Marston, North Carolina.

**Mukluk**: Eskimo winter boots made of animal hide and fur.

**Muktuk**: whale fat, an Eskimo delicacy.

**Muskeg**: tundra in the Aleutian Islands.

**NORAD**: North American Air Defense sites. These radar sites were established in the Alaska Interior to track incoming ICBMs and Soviet aircraft once they had been detected by the DEW sites.

**Oomiak:** large Eskimo boat traditionally constructed of walrus skin. In the Aleutians, the oomiak was called a biadarka or a bidar.

**Outside:** to an Alaskan, the Lower 48.

**Parka:** Eskimo winter jacket.

**Polynyas:** large, permanent open stretches of water in the ice pack. The polynyas are natural and could be formed by upwellings or warm water springs beneath the surface. A polynya is not a lead. A lead is a temporary open stretch of water, usually between two sheets of floating ice.

**Pontoons:** the large flotation devices for landing on water that many bush planes use instead of wheels.

**Promyshleniki:** Russian entrepreneurs who originally traded for furs with the Natives of Alaska before the sale of Alaska to the United States.

**Rail belt:** anywhere in Alaska between Seward and Fairbanks that has access to the Alaska Railroad.

**RATNET:** Rural Alaska Television Network, the state-owned television broadcast network. Today cable television is available in many communities.

**Ring of Fire:** the ring of lands and islands around the Pacific where volcanic activity is prevalent.

**Scramble:** when United States Air Force planes must take off to intercept incoming Soviet aircraft.

**Sourdough:** a seasoned Alaskan, one who had lived through a winter, from freeze-up to break-up.

**STOL:** Short Take Off and Landing, adaptations to bush planes that made it possible for them to land and take off from short landing strips.

**Taku:** a strong, violent winter wind in Southeast Alaska.

**Termination Dust:** the first snow of winter that dusts the tops of the mountains. It is called termination dust because it meant that many people would be terminating what they were doing and leaving Alaska before the deep snow and cold of winter came.

**Thousand Mile War:** the Second World War in the Aleutians with the Japanese holding one end of the island chain and the Americans the other.

**Tingmayuk:** Eskimo word for bird and also the name of the first plane to attempt to fly in Alaska.

**Tlingit-Haida-Tsimshian:** one of four ethnic groups in Alaska. These three closely-related peoples live in Southeast Alaska.

**Tropospheric scatter:** the practice of bouncing a communications beam off the troposphere, that belt of atmosphere 7 to 10 miles above the surface of the earth. It was known as a scatter because while the radio beam could be shot upwards in a tight beam, it scattered as it bounced down and had to be collected by huge antenna which resembled drive-in movie screens but were many times larger.

**Tundra:** Alaska swampland with many mosquitoes and low vegetation.

**Tundra tires:** large, apparently over-inflated tires used by bush planes to land on the tundra.

**To turn turtle:** a nautical term meaning to turn over, as in an overloaded ship would turn over in the water.

**Tundra Daisy**: a 55 gallon barrel. So many of these were abandoned in remote parts of Alaska that today the drum is nicknamed an Tundra Daisy because, as the old saying goes, "they sprout everywhere."

**Visqueen**: thick, black plastic that is usually used in sheets.

VOR: VHF omnidirectional range finder, a navigational aid that can find and lock onto a direction beam.

*This is one of the four WACOs owned by Northern Air Service. WACOs were very popular among cargo pilots because they could pack a heavy load—evidenced by the cargo here—and had large cargo doors so you could get everything inside. The pilot, Clarence J. Rhode, is on the far right. Rhode will go one to become the Federal Director of Fish and Wildlife. In 1958 he disappeared on a routine plane flight. Half a century later his plane was discovered by accident.* Photo courtesy of the University of Alaska Fairbanks.

**Wetland**: see tundra

**Williwaw**: a sudden, violent, unpredictable wind-and-storm system indigenous to the Aleutian Islands.

# BIBLIOGRAPHY

*ALASKA ALMANAC.* Alaska Northwest Publishing Company, 1988.

*ALASKA'S NATIVE PEOPLE.* Alaska Geographic, 1979.

Anchorage Centennial Commission, Aviation Committee. *100 ALASKA BUSH PILOTS.* 1967.

*BITS AND PIECES OF ALASKAN HISTORY* (two volumes), Alaska Northwest Publishing Company, 1982.

Brink, Frank. *Sounds of Alaska.* (record)

Bruder, Gerry. *HEROES OF THE HORIZON.* Alaska Northwest Books, 1991.

*BUSH PILOTS.* Time/Life Series.

Cernick, Cliff. *SKYSTRUCK: TRUE TALES OF AN ALASKA BUSH PILOT.* Alaska Northwest Books, 1989.

Chelnov, Jean Potter. *THE FLYING FRONTIERSMEN.* Macmillan, 1956.

Cloe, John Haile. *THE AIR FORCE IN ALASKA.* Office of History, Alaskan Air Command, April, 1986.

*THE ALEUTIAN WARRIORS.* Pictorial Histories, 1991.

Cohen, Stan. *FLYING BEATS WORK.* Pictorial Histories, 1988.

*THE FORGOTTEN WAR.* Volumes I, II, III, and IV. Pictorial Histories, 1988.

Cole, Dermot. *FRANK BARR: BUSH PILOT IN ALASKA AND THE YUKON.* Alaska Northwest Publishing Company, 1986.

Cole, Terrance. *It Never Got Off the Ground, Alaska-Yukon Magazine,* insert in *Alaska Magazine,* March, 1984, pages A-18 to A-20.

Day, Beth. *GLACIER PILOT.* Comstock, 1981.

Emmons, George Thornton Emmons. *THE TLINGIT INDIANS.* University of Washington Press, 1991.

Fejes, Claire. *VILLAGER.* Random House, 1981.

Garfield, Brian. *THE THOUSAND MILE WAR.* Bantam, 1969.

Greiner, James. *WAGER WITH THE WIND, THE DON SHELDON STORY.* Rand McNally, 1974.

*HANDBOOK OF NORTH AMERICAN INDIANS,* Volumes 4 and 5. Smithsonian, 1984.

Harkey, Ira. *PIONEER BUSH PILOT.* University of Washington, 1974.

Helmricks, Harmon. *THE LAST OF THE BUSH PILOTS.* Bantam, 1969.

Janson, Lone E. *MUDHOLE SMITH.* Alaska Northwest Publishing Company, 1981.

Jefford, Jack. *WINGING IT.* Rand McNally & Company, 1981.

Jones, Vernard E. *HOW I BECAME AN ALASKAN BUSH PILOT.* Carlton Press, 1983.

Krause, Aurel. T*HE TLINGIT INDIANS.* University of Washington, 1956.

Miller, Polly and Leon Gordon. *LOST HERITAGE OF ALASKA.* World Publishing, 1967.

Mills, Stephen E. *ARCTIC WAR BIRDS, ALASKA AVIATION OF WORLD WAR II.* Superior Publishing, 1971.

*SOURDOUGH SKY, A PICTORIAL HISTORY OF FLIGHTS AND FLYERS IN THE BUSH.* Superior Publishing Company, 1969.

Nelson, Edward William. *THE ESKIMO ABOUT THE BERING STRAIT.* Smithsonian, 1983.

Oswalt, Wendall H. *ALASKAN ESKIMO.* Chandler Press, 1967.

Potter, Jean. *THE FLYING NORTH.* Macmillan, 1945.

Ruotsala, James A. Various articles in *Air Alaska, Alaska Flying, Alaska People, Alaskan Southeaster Magazine* and *Alaska Exposure.*

Satterfield, Archie. *THE ALASKA AIRLINES STORY.* Alaska Northwest Publishing Company, 1981.

*ALASKA BUSH PILOTS IN FLOAT COUNTRY.* Superior Publishing Company, 1969.

Stevens, Robert W. *ALASKA'S AVIATION HISTORY.* Polynyas Press, 1990.

Wilson, Jack. *GLACIER WINGS AND TALES.* Great Northwest Publishing Company, 1988.

*This was Archie Ferguson's store and home in Kotzebue in 1945. It was formerly a United States Army Air Corp building. After the Second World War, abandoned military buildings were cannibalized all across Alaska. Ferguson insulated this building with sand. Note the bags in the foreground. They are full of coal. Kotzebue did not have a natural source of energy so coal had to be used and every chunk of coal had to be transported in by barge or Bush airplane.*
Courtesy of the University of Alaska Fairbanks.

# INDEX

## Symbols

## A

# N

# O

*This is a genuine Alaska Gold Rush dance hall. This dance hall, actually a saloon, was in Arctic City, one of the very few communities that had any power. If you look very closely at the moose head over the doorway you will see a wire and light bulb. Also take a good look at the rubber boots of the man on the far left. This picture was clearly taken in the Spring when all travel was on muddy trials. Also note that the two women. They are a far cry from the Hollywood version of the dance hall queens.* Photograph courtesy of the Anchorage Museum Rasmuson Center.